NOTHING.

...where love and deceit are on a collision path

...where love and deceit are on a collision path

Anurag Anand

Srishti
PUBLISHERS & DISTRIBUTORS

Srishti Publishers & Distributors
N-16, C. R. Park
New Delhi 110 019
srishtipublishers@gmail.com

First published by Srishti Publishers & Distributors in 2010

3rd impression, 2011

This is entirely a work of fiction. All characters and events are totally imaginary.

Typeset in AGaramond 11pt. by Suresh Kumar Sharma at Srishti

Printed and bound in India

Dedicated to: My Grandparents

I wish for my books to be half as gripping and fulfilling as those bed time stories that made me wait impatiently for the day to end and night to fall.

Acknowledgements

Chasing your destiny is not a vice...
As long as you know, what is the price?
This one goes out to you, my friends...
Running in a race that will never end.
Chasing success and driven by desire,
Whose house is it that you set on fire?

I thank my parents and my loving wife,
Your love and affection is how I thrive.
Words are written and words are read,
In the company of friends, stories are bred.
You stand by my side or time does us apart,
In shaping my stories, you will always play a part.

Ravi, for his continued guidance and advice,
My publisher for deciding to roll the dice,
Vinitha and Shaheen for their precious time,
This thank you is not only for the sake of rhyme.
And as you hold this book in your hand,
I welcome you too, my reader, to this fantasy land.

The First Lap – Mumbai (June '07)

The human vision is nothing but an augmentation of the subject's mental state. While a happy and content mind is capable of appreciating the exquisiteness in the panorama of abject poverty showcased on the streets of a metropolis like Mumbai, even it's grandeur and exuberance fails to catch the attention of a preoccupied mind.

It was about 9.40 p.m. when Akash pulled his Honda Civic in front of his apartment building. It normally took him all of twenty minutes to drive from his office in Santacruz to his rented apartment on Hill Road in Bandra West. But today he had been wedged in maddening traffic for over an hour and had not come across any apparent reason for the sudden assemblage of vehicles on the road. Not to mention the minor occurrence that had further accounted for about 15 minutes of his time, on the way.

After one of the many traffic signals on Turner Road turned green, Akash released the clutch, relieved to be on the move again. Just then, a taxi which was comfortably standing in the left lane decided to take a right turn, kissing the front bumper of Akash's Honda with his rear one. Lane driving is anyways a talent fast eroding from the streets of Mumbai and especially when it comes to taxis, the roads are hardly any safer than a predator crammed jungle.

Instinctively Akash followed, turning right himself and signaling for the taxi to stop. The driver complied and seemed apologetic to begin with. "My mistake sahib, but it is a small scratch, will go with a little scrubbing", he said.

"Yeah right. Do you have any idea how much the repair is going to cost me? And if a little scrubbing is all that is required, why don't you do that for me?" Akash replied. His temper somewhat allayed by the taxi driver's unexpectedly timid response. The damage had been done and the guilty party was obviously in no position to make good the loss. However, since the driver had questioned the severity of the damage, he signaled for him to get down from the car and inspect the bumper. *If there are any doubts about the damage he has done, he better see it for himself.* Some curious passerbys had stopped on the pavement, looking for their daily doze of free entertainment that the city roads never cease to offer.

The taxi driver complied and followed him, muttering some kind of an explanation for what had happened. The sight of the scratched bumper triggered something that Akash did not immediately comprehend. Suddenly, he was no longer the guilty party begging to be spared but an aggressive warrior, ready for a duel.

"This is not your Delhi that you expect me to pay for your car repairs. Such small things happen on Mumbai roads", he spoke in fluent Marathi. Though Akash had started to understand the language, his Marathi vocabulary was limited to the slogans written behind auto rickshaws that he was compelled to read when stuck in traffic jams and blurting out a "Mulgi shikli, pragati zaali (educate the girl child and ensure development)" or "Naitikta paala, AIDS taala (be principled and avoid AIDS)" was not going to establish him as a thoroughbred Marathi under the given circumstances.

"Hindi mein bol (speak in Hindi)", Akash replied, matching the taxi drivers pitch. It was the Delhi number plate on his car that had done the trick and the taxi driver who minutes ago was apologizing for his mistake in fluent Hindi had now shifted gears along with his language – an aggressive avatar intent on teaching the outsider a lesson.

"This is not your Delhi. I don't know Hindi, you speak in Marathi", the driver continued in Marathi glancing at the people assembled on the nearby pavement from the corner of his eye.

A local party claiming to be the savior of the Marathi populace had recently raked the issue of North Indians migrating to Maharashtra and taking up majority of the better paying jobs. In the age of meritocracy, where talent and competency are touted to be the sole determinants of an individual's success, this distorted logic had still found fervor with some locals and the taxi driver was using it to his full advantage.

Akash was outraged and it was no longer because of his scratched car. He was furious at the conniving taxi driver for giving the entire incident a lingual and regional shade only to avoid admitting his mistake. It was the first time that he was feeling like an outsider in his own country and it felt worse than the Monday morning meetings, where his boss did not hesitate in giving people a piece of his mind in the presence of the entire team. He wanted to respond, but he knew that the situation was delicate and he could not place high stakes on the prevailing sanity of the onlookers who were seemingly anxious in anticipation of some action.

"Yes, my dad bought Delhi so it is mine and your dad

bought Mumbai so it is yours. It is people like you who are responsible for the state the country is in today. You can never grow above being a taxi driver and will die one day taking all your sick thoughts with you", he blurted out, frustration getting the better of him.

Without waiting for a reaction, Akash sat in his car and drove off. In the background, he could hear the animated monologue of the taxi driver, who was informing the crowd that the game was over and he had won convincingly. The fading words sounded to him like the victory cries of a warlord whose valor had made the enemy flee from the battleground.

'The bastard could not find a better day to screw my happiness. Can't even make it to the gym on time now', he thought as he waited for the guard to arise from his sleepy existence and open the gates. It took three honks for a flicker of life to emerge in the stationary figure of the guard who took his time looking for his chappals, getting up from the chair, walking up to the gate and finally opening it for the car to get in. *'So slow these people are. They deserve what they get in life. Let the bugger come to me for his Diwali Baksheesh this time...'* he thought as he parked the car in its designated spot and headed for the building lift.

The lights in the apartment were switched off which meant that Deepali was yet to return from work. He reached for his laptop bag to take out the house keys when his mobile phone beeped. It was a text message from Deepali. 'Still in offc..will leave in abt ten mins,' the message read. *'Too busy to even type complete words',* he almost murmured while opening the door and reaching out for the electricity switch.

The apartment was tastefully done up with each room adorning a different theme echoed by the choice of colors used on the walls. The drawing room had white walls with black and white photographs forming a checkered design on one of them. The furniture consisted of a low settee, two polka dotted bean bags and a bar cabinet, all in dark shades, the contrast giving the room an ultra modern look. The 42" LED television set and the attached home theatre system added to the elegance.

The master bedroom had a blue theme with three walls painted in a light shade and the fourth in a darker shade of blue. The kitchen had a light look and feel with cream walls while the guest room was painted in yellow with one of the walls in a bright orange shade. The upholstery in all the rooms, ranging from the curtains to the bed sheets to the wall hangings matched with the walls. Akash dropped his laptop bag on the settee and slumped on one of the bean bags, reaching out for the television remote and kicking off his shoes in a single synchronized motion.

The aroma hanging in the air suggested that the cook had already prepared dinner and left, but he was in no mood to eat just as yet. After flipping through the channels and not coming across anything that could hold his attention, he lazily got up, walked to the balcony and picked up the towel that was hanging on the clothes line along with the clothes he had washed on Monday. Peevishly, he threw the towel on his shoulder, reaching out for the other clothes, giving them some respite from the three days of importunate hanging, dumping them on the bed in the guest room.

Normally, both Akash and Deepali did their washing over the weekends. When one of them would put their clothes in the machine during the week, invariably they would remain there for a couple of days and if they were taken out on time and put in the balcony to dry, they would remain there till such time that either of them returned in time from work to catch the 'press walah' during his visit to the complex.

It was over the weekend that they also did their weekly shopping for rations and cleaned the house. The clean up was a tedious process comprising of putting everything from clothes, books, documents, newspapers, footwear and utensils that had been used during the week, back in their original place. Though a maid came in every morning, her job description was limited to wiping the floors and cleaning utensils. She didn't believe in the theory of customer delight and never made an attempt to venture into any task that would help with the upkeep of the apartment but had not been summarily assigned to her. As a result, just before the advent of any weekend, the apartment looked more like a bachelor's pad than a flat housing a high flying executive couple. Thankfully it was a Thursday and just one more day of work before yet another lazy weekend would dawn.

He took a shower and re-negotiated his position in front of the television set, hoping to find something that would grab his attention this time around. Interestingly, one of the Hindi news channels caught his fancy. The breaking news being aired on the channel had something to do with aliens stealing cows from poor villagers and taking them to their own planets for worshipping.

'An adult's answer to cartoon network', Akash thought, smiling at the amateurish animation that had been used to show the cows vanishing from the streets and re-appearing amidst a host of flashing lights, switches and levers of all shapes and sizes, meant to resemble a spaceship. Suddenly the space ship started to make a loud shrilling noise and the lights began to flicker. The sound continued to increase in intensity till he could feel its vibrations inside his head.

Not being able to tolerate it any longer, he tried to shut his ears and in the process realized that he had dozed off sometime during the program and the shrilling noise was the door bell of his apartment. He glanced at the wall clock – 11.15 p.m., and ambled towards the door.

"You were sleeping? Had aunty (the cook) come? You had your dinner?" Deepali walked in, assaulting the sleepy soul with a barrage of questions. Akash slumped back on the settee without bothering to answer any of them, fighting a strong desire to hit the bed and go back to a world that he knew would not demand much of him.

Deepali took about 10 minutes to change into her house clothes and by then Akash had found a television reality show to keep him occupied. "I told you I was getting late, you should have eaten", she said as she set the meal on the table.

"You never told me anything except for a text message that said you were leaving office. And that too was about an hour and half back", Akash replied serving himself the barely edible food that the cook had prepared. "Plus, I wasn't really hungry."

One would have expected this conversation to result in another domestic quarrel or at least a bit of sulking, but three years of marriage had taught them better than to blow such small matters out of proportion. The next five minutes went in complete silence, both of them totally focused on the contents of their respective plates. "I have some international visitors coming in next week and need to prepare a presentation for them. Have completed the first draft today but I am sure Mr. 'Know it all' will have his bits to add tomorrow", she said, referring to her boss. "How was your day?"

"My day was ok, except that I would have loved to kill a few people if I could help it", Akash replied without looking up from his plate. By the time they completed their dinner, he had narrated the entire incident involving the taxi driver to her. "These people, they should all be thrown behind bars."

"Relax, why are you boiling your blood over some stupid uneducated fellow? I hope the car is not damaged much, and thank god that you didn't get hurt", she responded in an effort to calm him down.

"Boiling my blood? I wish I could.... I could... huff"

"Let it be. You should not react so much to such small incidents", she continued.

"Small incident? Yaar, forget it. You will never understand" he said as he got up from the dinner table and walked towards the bedroom. By the time Deepali cleared the dining table, put the utensils in the sink and came to the bedroom, Akash was sound asleep. Another typical day in their lives had come to an end.

The origin of the institution of marriage can be traced back to the need of a secure environment for the perpetuation of species in the primitive societies. Over centuries, this practice of binding two individuals in the nuptial knot has evolved in every society inhabited by humans. From being a sacred and religious bond to being a means for financial gain (dowry), from grand ceremonies for the selection of the right bride or groom to the practice of marrying multiple times (polygamy), this institution has found its place in all communities, albeit in different forms and dictated by varying social norms.

The most prevalent form of marital alliance in the modern and progressive segments of the Indian society of today is the one that is termed as 'love marriage'. The intensity or in some cases even the very existence of love might be questionable but in a nutshell this refers to an alliance where the boy and girl meet, decide that they are the right partners for each other, convince their parents (at least in some cases) and get married. Four simple steps to a lifetime of pain and pleasure, smooth progress and quivering turbulence. Akash and Deepali were no different. They had complied with the norms of their generation and fallen in love before tying the marital knot, marking the beginning of a life filled with hope, love and happiness; the not-so-secret ingredients of a successful marriage.

Starting Line – Back To School (September '01 to March '02)

The scornful set of events that unfolded on September 11, 2001 impacted thousands of lives across the globe. Be it the plight of those who had relatives and friends working at the World Trade Center or the horror that millions experienced watching the twin icons of modern capitalism crumbling down on their television sets, the event had resulted in widespread gloom and despair. In addition to those who were directly impacted by this act of terrorism, a host of others got engulfed in the aftermath which resulted in an economic recession across the globe.

Companies were shut down, jobs were cut, investments were pulled out and visa norms for most western destinations were tightened. This, coupled with the recent bursting of the Dot Com Bubble spelt doom for India Inc, which was still trying to find its footing in the global economic framework. The situation was anything but favorable, especially if you were a final year student of a 'non top ten' B-School (Business School) in India, eagerly awaiting your grand entry into the corporate world.

In fact the situation was more like the thrill of riding a high speed elevator suddenly cut short by a shuddering halt coupled with the sound of snapping wires. The soaring aspirations had been cut short and the desire to scale new heights had given way to a desperate attempt to cling on to dear life instead. Individual goals had been realigned from the ambitious to the more basic ones; in this case, getting any decent job befitting an MBA tag.

This sense of obscurity seemed to be precipitating all around Akash. The animated discussions in the canteen had given way to serious chit-chats with concerned undertones. Fear seemed to have taken a toll on the hundred odd students who until a few months back were bubbling with enthusiasm and optimism. The emotion of fear, as it always does, resulted in different reaction from different people. While some seemed to be buckling down under pressure and had started to look for ways to shield themselves, others had intensified their vivacity to seize control.

Safety and control, though at times mutually independent, are the two emotions said to help in successfully countering fear. So, while some of his classmates were revising their optimistic career preferences to more realistic ones, Akash had found a renewed vigor to take control of his destiny in the wake of the unfavorable circumstances.

"HLL has also declined to come to campus this year," Vikram, a close friend of Akash and a member of the placement committee informed him over a bottle of beer. Both of them shared a common penchant for Marketing and wanted to start their careers with an FMCG or an advertising company. This common thread had bound them together very early during their days at the campus and they invariably squeezed time from the plethora of assignments and submissions to have a peaceful drink romanticizing about the corporate world and all that it had in store for them.

"This is getting nowhere. By the time the placement week commences we would be lucky to have even one FMCG company coming to campus," Vikram continued. "I wish they would pull the maniac out from hiding, dragging him by the beard and feed him to a bunch of hungry… jobless MBA's."

"Any news on our resumes that you had sent to the alumni working with FMCG companies?" Akash enquired, fully aware of the answer that he would get. If there had been positive news from any possible quarter, Vikram could not have held it back for so long.

"No, absolutely nothing."

A thoughtful pause followed. It was 10.30 pm and beyond the open window of Vikram's room, the cold November night was bracing the city in a cloudy blanket of fog. The chilly winters of Delhi and cold beer might not be the favored permutation for many, but hostel life is known to be governed by its own set of idiosyncrasies. The choice of drink, just like the brand of cigarettes and the selection of seats in a movie theatre, is governed by the single most important factor called money. As the month and hence the monthly allowance starts to deplete, the dearer indulgences start making way for the more affordable ones and a pack of Marlboro cigarettes finds itself aptly substituted by a bundle of the local *bidi.* Hence, when Vikram had decided to pay a visit to the local liquor shop after dinner, he had inspected his wallet and consequently settled for two bottles of beer instead of a bottle of the more expensive Rum.

"And imagine, these fools are still working diligently on their assignments. As if once the submissions are made public, the corporates will be stamping each others toes to employ them," Vikram's frustration was now directed towards his fellow classmates, most of whom had retired to their rooms by now. "I know what you mean, but not all of them are as worried as we are. Most of them will eventually join their family business and the degree will only help secure more dowry when their families decide to encash them. And then there are the likes of Dipish, whose dad will get him a better paying job than anything that the campus could have got him in the best of times. So, that just leaves people like us to do something about our situation."

"But what else can we do?" Vikram said more as a reaction to Akash's exaggerated statement than a question.

"Why can't we? Why can't we approach some of these companies directly and try and speak to the HR or the Marketing Managers? Who knows, someone might just decide to grant us an interview. Isn't that all we need?"

"Have you lost it? The Placement Committee is in touch with every possible company that has even the remotest chance of recruiting this year. Why do you think the companies will say a no for coming to the campus and instead agree to call us for an interview? And more importantly, what if the institute comes to know about this? Do you realize, we could be debarred from the placement week?"

"I know there is a risk. But who has the time in the corporate world to complain to the institute about two students seeking a job. At best they would turn us down. What have we got to lose? And anyways, as you said, none of the FMCG companies are likely to make it to campus, so what will the placement week have to offer to us?" Akash's arguments were persuasive and made sense. Soon Vikram's aspirations managed to overpower the conformist within and the discussion shifted from strategic to the tactical aspects.

A plan of action was drawn. Over the next couple of days both of them would individually compile a list of relevant companies in Gurgaon and try and fix up appointments for Saturday since it was the only day that they did not have any lectures and could afford to completely devote to their endeavor.

The data collection was a piece of cake and with the internet lending a helping hand it didn't take Akash much time to prepare a list of 12 companies, complete with their board line numbers and addresses. However, the start of a journey is not always the best indicator of its end. It just took a few telephone calls for him to realize the enormity of the task they had embarked upon. The telephone operators who took his calls seemed to be holding a grudge against mankind in general and Akash in particular; trained to the 'T' in making the caller realize his worth (or the lack of it) without for a minute deviating from their sugar coated tones. "I am sorry sir, I would not be able to connect you to anyone unless you give me a name and an extension number," and "What is this regarding? Sorry, he is traveling for the entire week," were the standard responses he got.

Things were not very different with Vikram. "These bloody

receptionists think of themselves as no less than the CEO of the company. I wonder if they are equally stubborn at home. Remind me never to get married to one," he summed up when Akash enquired about his progress. Their optimism was fast draining but neither of them had the nerve to suggest cancelling the plan to the other.

As they zipped towards their destination on Saturday morning, they had more reasons than one to thank their stars. Vikram's motorbike had started without a fuss and not broken down as yet. Though they had decided to skip breakfast, the eventuality of bumping into a few other students while getting out of campus could not be ruled out, and since they didn't have a satisfactory explanation for their formal attire, they were glad to be able to sneak out unnoticed. The traffic was leaner than expected and they made it to the Delhi – Gurgaon border with enough time to make a small halt for breakfast. The cups of tea and bread omelets served at the roadside stall had been delightfully fulfilling.

Their first destination was Global Towers, a multi-storied building that housed over 30 companies, six of them featuring between the two lists that they had drawn up. The lobby was grand with a large open area followed by a passage which had three elevators on either side, facing each other. A large wooden board listed down the names of the offices on each of the floors for the benefit of visitors. There were a total of fifteen floors and while some larger companies had entire floors to themselves, some floors housed as many as four offices. The top floor belonged to a large confectionary company that had found a mention in both their lists, so it was decided that they would start with the fifteenth floor and walk their way down, tapping all relevant offices on the way.

"Good morning Ma'm," Akash wished the receptionist with a smile that stretched a few millimeters beyond his usual one. Nevertheless, the effort went down in vain as the frown that was there on her face remained intact when she looked up towards them. "Yes?" she enquired, without acknowledging the greeting. "We are final year MBA students from IBA Business School and we would like to meet the HR Manager," Akash continued, persisting with his smile.

"Do you have an appointment?" her tone and the sudden question wiped off the smile instantly. "No. But we just needed 5 minutes of his time to check if there are any relevant openings that we could be considered for," he replied. "He will not meet you without an appointment. What you can do is, leave your bio-datas with me and I will pass them on to him. He will call you back if there is something," she suggested, not leaving a scope for any further dialogue. They gave her copies of their resume and proceeded to the next floor, without a doubt that the HR Manager was never in his life going to set eyes on the sheets of paper they had left behind. "I didn't know they were still using the word, bio-data," Akash commented, in an unsuccessful attempt to hide his anguish and embarrassment.

Two more attempts and they realized that it would take something out of the ordinary for them to break this wall called the receptionist and manage a meaningful conversation with somebody more significant. "Out of the box thinking," their Strategic Management professor would say, "is what differentiates the successful managers from the rest." If there was a time to think out of the box, it was now. A revised reactive strategy was quickly formulated on the staircase between the 13th and the 14th floor of Global Towers. Vikram wasn't totally convinced but since Akash had come up with the idea, he gladly consented to witness it being tested. The hatrick of rejections had drained Vikram of his enthusiasm, so he opted for the safer bet of letting Akash do what he had to rather than getting into another debate.

The office they walked into next was that of a major player in the Consumer Durables space. The receptionist seemed as mechanical as the other three they had encountered so far. Akash confidently approached her desk, Vikram in tow and asked to see the Marketing Manager. One hand still holding the telephone receiver that she had just picked up, she gave them a lazy glance and asked, "Regarding?"

"We are from IBA. This is regarding a report on the impact of the polarization of wealth on the economic framework with a special emphasis on the durables sector. We would like some comments from him. It would hardly take 5 minutes." The jargon had thoroughly confused her as intended and all she could gather was that they were two important people wanting to discuss something equally important. Akash had deliberately left the words, "Business School" out of his introduction leaving the institutions core area of functioning open to her interpretation.

She took the telephone receiver she was holding, closer to her ears and dialed a number. "Sir, there are a couple of other visitors who would want to see you for 5 minutes regarding a report," they heard her attempting to explain the purpose of their visit to the person on the other end of the line. His response was short and the receiver still sticking to her ears she signaled towards the seats in the waiting area. "Five minutes," she said, continuing with the strict rationing of the number of words she spoke.

Akash was exhilarated at the success of the plan but avoided an eye contact with Vikram for the fear of giving the receptionist any clues about the true purpose of their visit as they walked towards the two empty seats on one side of the hall. "Hey, you guys are from IBA Business School?" a person sitting on one of the chairs facing them, casually enquired. The question startled them and they looked at each other like two burglars returning from a successful outing only to be apprehended for questioning by an unsuspecting cop on beat duty. Akash stole a quick glance in the direction of the receptionist and finding her engrossed in a telephonic conversation, looked back at the man and replied in the affirmative.

"Oh that's neat," he continued, oblivious to their discomfort. "I am also an IBA pass out, 97 batch," he said with a pleasant smile. "That's nice. So where are you working currently?" Akash enquired, more out of courtesy than interest. He introduced himself as Rishi, an Account Director with a leading advertising agency. Amongst other clients, he handled the account of this company as well and was here for a briefing. "So, what is the project that you guys have come here for?" he continued with his intrusion. But just as Akash started to respond, the door connecting the main office floor to the reception area opened and a smart looking man of about 32 to 35 years walked towards Rishi.

Akash was glad that the conversation had been cut short as Rishi got up to greet the newcomer. "Hi Rishi, I hope you didn't have to wait for long?" he said.

"No, I just came in about five minutes back,"

"Who else is here to see me?" he enquired, looking in the direction of the receptionist who in turn signaled towards the chairs occupied by Akash and Vikram.

"If you don't mind, can I just take another five minutes to meet with these gentlemen?" he addressed Rishi, looking towards the two of them who had already got up from their seats. "Sure," Rishi said as he slumped back on his chair.

The meeting started off well, with Akash and Vikram taking turns to ask a set of made up questions for their hypothetical project. The answers they got were generic, but Vikram kept taking notes diligently. Just as he completed answering the fourth and the last of the questions, Akash decided to come to the point. "Sir, our placement week is due next month, but your company will not be participating this year. We are very keen to start our careers with an organization like yours and were wondering if there are any openings that we could apply for," he said, trying to make it sound as nonchalant as he could. "Well, all campus recruitments are handled by HR and as of now I don't think there are any openings in Marketing. Anyways, you can e-mail me your CV's and I shall let you know if anything comes up," he said, picking up his diary which signaled the conclusion of the meeting. They took his visiting card and walked out of the office as Rishi got up from his chair for the second time within a span of five minutes.

Their luck wasn't really riding on a high tide and the rest of the day did not yield any fruitful results. By 4.30 p.m., when they decided to head back to campus, they had visited about 28 offices; left behind 12 copies each of their resumes; collected 8 visiting cards; but were not confident of receiving even a single interview call. The experience had drained them of their motivation and another attempt of a similar nature was out of the question. Though they followed up with some of the companies they had met over the following weeks, nothing concrete emerged out of it.

It was the first day of the Placement Week and Vikram had just called to say that he had received his offer letter from an international insurance company that had recently set shop in India. Akash was happy for him but with the call, a sudden sinking feeling had started to creep into his system. He tried to suppress it as he waited for the list of short listed candidates from the first round interview of a pharmaceutical company that he had appeared for. As the time went by and the news of more and more classmates getting placement offers started to pour in, the feeling continued to intensify as if there was a parasitical ball of lead in his belly, feasting on his interiors and growing in size.

The list that he was waiting for eventually came out and only two candidates were short listed for the personal interview; he was not one of them. This news only worsened his mental state and finding it difficult to contain his conflicting emotions, he decided to retreat to the privacy of his hostel room. As much as he told himself that his anxiety was a result of not clearing the first round of the interview, somewhere deep within he knew that it had a lot to do with the excitement of his other class mates who had managed to get placed. '*Why didn't I decide to try for a financial services company instead? They have given out more number of offers and the better paying ones. Maybe I would have made it,'* he was thinking as he walked towards the hostel, fully aware that the heaviness and sinking feeling would only grow in the solitary confines of his room. The thought of being alone in the room was unnerving but he needed to vent out his emotions and couldn't be seen crying in public, especially given the celebratory mood all around.

As he was reaching out for the keys, his mobile phone rang again. The number was an unknown one, which meant that thankfully it was not another one of his classmates calling him to share the excitement of getting a job offer. "Hello," he said, making an effort to sound his usual self. "Hello. Is this Akash Malhotra?" the caller enquired.

"Yes, Akash here."

"Hi Akash. Rishi this side. We had met a couple of weeks back at one of my client's offices in Gurgaon," he continued.

"Yes of course. How are you doing Rishi?" Akash had managed to place Rishi but was puzzled about the reason for the call. More importantly, he couldn't recollect having shared his mobile number with him.

"I am fine, Thank you. Is this a good time to talk? I hope I didn't catch you in the middle of something?"

Yes, you did. You caught me in the middle of a mind fuck that is likely to leave me unemployed for the rest of my life. "No, no. You didn't. Please go ahead," he replied.

"The other day when we met up, Amit, the Marketing Manager seemed fairly impressed by you. In addition to your self confidence, I guess it was your method of approaching him that was impressive and made him share with me, the details of your meeting. I remembered about it when I was screening a few candidates for an opening on my team. So, I asked Amit for your resume and thought of calling you up. If you are interested in a client servicing role, we can meet up for a formal discussion on this," he said.

Interested...would a drowning man be interested in the sight of a lifeboat? Hell, yes. "It was really nice of you to think of me. Thank you. Yes, I would be keen to explore the option and can come down to meet you at your convenience."

"Can you make it to my office by about 11.00 a.m. tomorrow?"

Akash had another interview lined up at 3.00 the next day which left him with just enough time to meet up with Rishi. "Sure, I will be there at 11.00."

"Fine, see you tomorrow. But let me warn you, we might not be able to offer the kind of packages that some of the other companies on your campus would be offering. So, think it through and come only if you can defer your desire for a wardrobe with Armanis and Guccis for a few years." Akash laughed at the attempted humor but it was only later that he realized the true implications of this statement. Stuffing his wardrobe with Armanis would not take a few years but more than a few lifetimes with the kind of package he started his corporate career with. However, he was not complaining.

The Second Lap – The Corporate World (April '02 to May '03)

"Advertising is the art of creating dreams. It is a stimulus for changing thoughts and generating the desired response from a sizeable population of target customers. In our day to day functioning we sometimes become so overwhelmed by the timelines, client expectations and the need to achieve our targets that we tend to relegate our role to being a factory for churning out creatives. We forget that unless we add value to the brief that we get from our clients, we will continue to remain third party vendors for them and will never be able to partner with them in their success. It is only when we are able to partner with our clients in achieving their business objectives that we achieve success as an agency and you achieve success as a professional." The COO (Chief Operating Officer) of the agency continued with his induction address to the batch of functional trainees who had been recently recruited.

The batch comprised of nine people who had joined from various campuses and were to take up their roles in the agency's offices in Delhi and Mumbai. Five of the nine, including Akash were to join the client servicing department, two would be a part of the creative team and one each would be joining the art department and the strategic planning division. During the formal introductions, Akash learnt that majority of the batch had been recruited from an institution in Ahmedabad that offered a specialized post graduate course in Advertising and Communication. The only exceptions were Nikhil, an IIM – Lucknow graduate who was to join Strategic Planning, Gaurav – another MBA who was joining the Client Servicing team in Mumbai and Deepali – a Post Graduate in Mass Communications from Delhi University, who was joining the creative team.

The fact that five of the nine people came from the same campus meant a natural sub-division of the group and during the breaks in between sessions, Akash, by default found himself in the company of Nikhil, Gaurav and Deepali. A few familiar faces can do wonders in making someone comfortable in an alien environment, but Akash did not have this luxury. So while the other group seemed to be at ease with each other, he was still struggling to remember all the names that had been thrown at him since the morning.

After graduating from his campus, Akash had to look for an accommodation and shift out of the secure confines of the hostel. He had settled for a one room apartment in Gurgaon which was barely a few kilometers from his new office. The Bajaj Pulsar motorcycle that his father had given him as a graduation gift was turning out to be a lifeline in Gurgaon – a city plagued by the conspicuous absence of any kind of public transport. The first day of his induction concluded at 8.15 p.m. and Akash was glad to be heading towards his new dwelling. His first day at work had left him with mixed feelings and he wanted to be alone to take stock of his situation.

The information overdose had left him tired and he hadn't even got down to understanding his specific profile as yet. He was excited about his initiation into the corporate world and embarking on a journey towards an independent life but he could also feel a nervous sensation arise within him at the thought of getting back to office the next day. *Every successful career has to start somewhere, these are just the initial jitters and I should be fine soon.*

Just as a wild beast born and bred in the confines of a city zoo would learn to survive when left to foible in a jungle; Akash took no time in overcoming his jitters and adjusting to the new set of surroundings. He took to the workplace like his natural habitat - a place where he was always meant to be. Over the next couple of weeks, Rishi introduced Akash to the two clients he was expected to handle and took him through the kind of work that the agency had done on those accounts in the past. Rishi's job was simply to interact with the clients on a regular basis, understand their creative requirements and liaise with the internal creative team to ensure timely delivery. *Simple, indeed.*

It was only with time that the inherent conflict that came with every client facing job started to surface. The unrealistic expectations, the 'I know my product best' attitude and the continuous follow-ups required to get payments released made the task of servicing the clients that much more difficult. Then there were the internal roadblocks that had to be countered. The creative guys who took any critical feedback on their produce a little too personally; the finance team who seemed to be scared that the clients might suddenly wind up their business and vanish into oblivion and hence demanded that all invoices be accounted for within 15 days of them being raised; and not to mention, the boss, who always seemed dissatisfied with the monthly billings for each and every account. *The only thing left to be done is to design personalized name plates for all client employees and charge them a bomb for it. How on earth can I increase the billing when the clients know exactly the number of creative elements they require for their campaigns?*

"Akash, would it be possible for you to drop by to our office at about 5.00 p.m today?" It was Prarthna, the Marketing Manager from one of Akash's accounts, a telecommunications company. He involuntarily glanced at his wrist. *2.00 p.m., there goes the rest of the day.* Without waiting for an answer, Prarthna continued, "We have a foreign delegation visiting next week and I need to brief you on some creatives for elements to be put up in the office. It is slightly urgent." *Yeah urgent, like the last time and the time before that. As if I have an option.*

"Sure, I will see you at 5.00 in your office", he confirmed.

The meeting with Prarthna went as expected. Their global marketing head was visiting India on the coming Tuesday and the list of elements that were to be showcased ranged from the creatives for the upcoming promotional campaign, a brief for which had been shared with the agency just a couple of days back to a collage of all recent marketing initiatives that was to be put up in the reception area. *Does she realize that it is Thursday already? And the visit couldn't have been confirmed just today. Well, I am sure she has more important things to worry about than us agency folks having to burn the proverbial midnight oil. What a bitch.* After showing a mild dissent on the unrealistic timelines, Akash had no option but to agree to deliver. After all, she was the client.

Rishi was out for the entire week, attending a global conference in Greece. *'Lucky bugger,'* he thought as he mounted his bike and headed back to office. By the time Akash reached the Delhi – Gurgaon border, it was already 6.15 pm and the roads were swarmed with vehicles ferrying the luckier lot back home after another day at work. It took him another twenty minutes to negotiate the traffic and reach his office. The first challenge at hand was to explain his predicament to the creative director and make him agree to share the first cut creatives by the next afternoon. This would mean an unexpected late night for him and some of his team members and would certainly be faced with a fair degree of resistance. *It would all have been so much simpler had Rishi been around.*

"Hey, your body clock has gone for a toss or what? Coming into office when it is time to head back home?" It was Deepali. She was walking towards the reception, ready to head back home. "No yaar. Was out for a client visit, have just come back…needed to catch up with Anurag on some urgent stuff. You're heading home?"

"Well, I guess your urgent work with Anurag will have to wait till tomorrow. It is his daughter's birthday today and he has planned a get together at his place. Most of the team would already be half sloshed by now." She said, with a smile. "I got caught up with something so couldn't leave with them. In fact I am on my way there now, and if you don't have other plans, why don't u come along too?"

"What? You mean the entire creative team is out?"

"Yes. Not many people I know here who would prefer work over a free drink. The entire team left sometime back", her nonchalant tone was a stark contrast to the anxiety that was building up within him. "I am dead" were the only words he could utter.

"Why what happened? What is so critical that it can't wait till the morning?" she inquired, some concern finally creeping into her tone. "My clients have their global marketing team visiting early next week and they need like a zillion creatives for it. And guess what? They need to see the first cut versions for all of them by tomorrow."

"Oh, that sounds bad, but I am sure if we start early tomorrow we should be able to come out with something by the end of the day."

"I wish it were so simple. Their India management team needs to see all the creatives by tomorrow evening since they would not be working over the weekend. You know how finicky these people tend to get over such visits from the senior management.

In the end, it will be us who will be expected to make the changes they suggest over the weekend and deliver the final output by Monday. God, I hate my job" the desperation was evident in his voice.

"I understand Akash and I really wish I could help, but you know how it is. I can't start working on any creatives until the brief has been run past Anurag," she remarked sympathetically. Little did she know that her remark had sparked a ray of hope that Akash would cling on to. "You know what, you can actually help me. We can work on the creatives together right now and in the morning, I could share the brief with Anurag. I am sure he will understand the urgency."

"What? Have you lost it? It is 7.00 pm already. Plus, there is a party at my boss's place and my entire team is there. What will I tell him? That I didn't come for the party as I was working on some creatives that he hadn't even approved? You want me to lose my job or something?" Her concerns were valid but they soon got overpowered by the urge to help a colleague in distress. For the next 4 to 5 hours, they were working together on creatives for posters and signages, promoting prepaid mobile connections. It was almost midnight when they decided to call it a day.

The session had been fruitful and a lot of quality work had been accomplished; Akash was back to breathing normally. Unlike some of the other creative guys, Deepali had been open to Akash's suggestions allowing for continuous improvement on the 'work in progress' creatives and he in turn was sure that the output would be in line with the clients' expectations.

Deepali lived with her parents in Lajpat Nagar and since it was late in the night, Akash dropped her home, stopping enroute for dinner at the roadside 'paratha wallah' at AIIMS. By the time he could return back to his flat, there were barely a few hours left before he had to get up again. However, thanks to Deepali, he could now afford to catch some sleep within those few hours.

The first thing that Akash did the next morning was to send an e-mail to Rishi. Rishi would be accessing e-mails on his Blackberry and Akash wanted to keep him informed, lest his sense of urgency in getting the job done raked up some unwanted controversy in office. Anurag however was sympathetic to the entire episode and his cooperation ensured that the required creatives were shared with the client by early evening. Maybe, the appreciative e-mail that Rishi had sent to Deepali, marking a copy to Anurag and the branch head had something to do with it, but Akash was relieved.

Since Deepali had got voluntarily engaged with the assignment, she continued to work on it and the few minor changes that Prarthna required were taken care of on Saturday. Officially, the agency worked five days a week but it was seldom that Akash had found any noticeable difference in attendance on Saturdays. In all probability Deepali would have been in office anyways on that particular Saturday, but since it was Akash's assignment that she was working on, he felt somewhat guilty and to express his gratitude, invited her out for dinner. A connection that was established over posters meant to promote mobile connections was to go a long way and this was only the first of their many dates to come.

Deepali wasn't a conventional beauty and would not make heads turn on the Delhi streets; and a girl who does not get unwanted attention in the streets of Delhi would surely get lost in the crowd in any other metro city of the country. She had a wheatish complexion with long black hair that almost touched her waistline. A few kilos lighter and she could boast of having a fabulous figure, but for now she would be placed in the 'pleasantly plump' category. She had nice cute features, but they only added confusion to her appearance. She was stuck somewhere between the cute girl next door and the dusky siren look. Her simple wardrobe comprising mainly of Punjabi suits did not help in clearing the confusion.

It was when people got to know her better that the appeal of her personality inconspicuously surfaced. Beneath the cute and blasé façade was a determined and ambitious girl who was extremely focused on what she wanted to accomplish. She came from a middle class business family and had seen enough hardships in life to realize the importance of a progressive career and a financially independent life. Though her parents had tried their level best to give her all that she desired, she had understood the ups and downs of her father's garment business early in life and often refrained from expressing desires that would challenge them financially. When her friends in college boasted of the branded replicas they carried for handbags, she would not once voice the desire to replace her old handbag that she had picked up from one of the roadside stalls in Central Market. This compassion and understanding had now become a second nature to her and the sense of comfort she exhibited about being herself made her an extremely pleasant person for company.

She had humorous anecdotes to share on every possible topic and more importantly could lodge a smile on Akash's face even when he was in the most somber of moods. It was just a matter of time before Akash started looking forward to spending more and more time with her. Though both of them avoided any atypical interaction in office, Akash ensured that he dropped her home whenever he got the chance and on the way they would stop by at Barista for a cup of coffee or simply go on a drive towards the international airport and watch airplanes take off and land.

Akash continued to approach work with utmost sincerity and

dedication delivering to the best of his ability and after a year and a half, was rewarded with the addition of one more account to his portfolio. *Do your job well without complaining and people, instead of recognizing your efforts, feel that there is scope to laden you with more work. Weird are the ways of this world.* "It is just a matter of time before you are promoted to the post of an Account Manager, having your own team and a set of independent accounts to manage. Keep up the good work," Rishi said during his appraisal.

The going was good but not without its fair share of hiccups. Sometimes it would be the attitude exhibited by one of his clients and sometimes the internal office politics that would get on to his nerves. It was during such times that he needed Deepali the most. "You take things a little too seriously. Why bother about something that is not going to impact your life in any significant fashion?" she would casually remark before shifting the conversation to some obscure topic from the latest Bollywood blockbuster to global warming. By now he had decoded this ploy and her naïve attempts to make him forget his woes invariably succeeded in making him smile; more because of her sincerity than the effect of the diversion itself.

It was in one of his moments of frustration that Akash had decided to upload his resume on one of the job portals. He had forgotten all about it till he got a call from a consultant about an opening in Marketing with an FMCG company based out of Mumbai. "There is no harm in trying. Whether to take it up or not is a decision that would need to be pondered over much later," Deepali had suggested. The prospect of sitting on the client's side of the table was enticing and FMCG was a sector where all the action was – the hefty media and communication budgets and the fiercely competitive environment. Akash had an initial telephonic round, post which he was summoned to Mumbai for the final interview. This was the first time that he was visiting Mumbai and the city did not exactly capture his imagination. The narrow and overcrowded roads, the extra humidity in the air, it was indeed a contrast to Delhi - a city he had grown to love. *To hell with it. Half a day is hardly enough to make up my mind about the entire city. Plus, I am not exactly moving here just as yet.*

The interview went off well and Akash returned to Delhi, hopeful of being extended a job offer soon. "They have met a few other candidates as well and should be closing on the position within a couple of days. The feedback about you was positive and I will keep you posted once I hear from them," the consultant had said.

Over a week had passed since his trip to Mumbai and just when his hopes had started to dwindle, the consultant called him again. He had made it. They were willing to make an offer and wanted his current salary details, basis which his compensation package would be worked out. Akash was elated. That evening he took Deepali to Buzz, one of the trendiest bars in Gurgaon. He had special news to break and it called for a special celebration.

"What's with your mood today? Got the results of your interview or what?' were the first words she spoke as they were ushered to their table. *So much so for the surprise and the breaking news.*

"How do you happen to know everything? Yes, I have got the job and wait till you hear the package that they are offering,' his excitement was more than evident.

"Wow. That's super cool," she said, getting up to give him a hug. He went on to share the details of his new role and the salary that he would be drawing while she listened intently. "And when do they want you to join?" she asked. "At the earliest possible. I intend to have a word with Rishi the first thing tomorrow morning and depending on how soon I can be relieved, I shall negotiate for my date of joining."

"So, this is about the end of your stint in Delhi?" she continued with her quizzing; only this time her volume was much lower and she sounded somewhat staid. It was then, that a sudden realization dawned upon Akash, something that he had missed thinking about amidst the excitement of getting a new, better paying job. The end of his stint in Delhi would also mean the end for the two of them, the end of the coffees at Barista, the end of a friendship that had become such an integral part of him that he had almost started taking it for granted. How often is it that the fear of losing something we thought as always being ours, redefines its entire worth for us?

The sudden feeling of loss had dwarfed all the excitement that he had been holding up since the morning. "Why don't you also come along?" he managed to utter after a few minutes of nervous silence. "Come where Akash? I have my job, my family. What do I tell them? Please don't get me wrong, this is a fabulous break and I am extremely happy for you. Mumbai is not too far away; we will keep in touch and remain the best of friends. Now stop mourning and cheer up," she said, gently placing her hand on his and forcing a smile. *Always the selfless one, trying to cheer me up even at the expense of suppressing her own feelings. What will I ever do without her?*

"Well, I have an idea. Why don't we get married?"

"What? Are you by any chance proposing to me?" She did well to sound surprised, but the underlying happiness could not be concealed.

"Well, I wasn't exactly prepared for this. But yes, I guess we can call this a proposal," he said, searching for something apt before settling for the napkin on their table, folding it awkwardly to resemble what he later explained to be a rose and getting down on his knees. Deepali burst out laughing, "Stop it, will you?" she said, pulling the napkin from his outstretched hand. "I will stop, but first, will you marry me?"

"I thought you would never ask. Yes, of course," she said holding his hands and pulling him towards her. "God. Can't they have carpets or something on the floor, this thing is painful," he playfully remarked, before they embraced for their first lip lock which lasted long enough for them to forget everything around them – the blaring music, the patrons occupying the other tables, their office and Akash's impending shift to Mumbai.

The next couple of weeks were extremely hectic for Akash. Rishi had not accepted his resignation and had in turn offered him a promotion; an attempt to make him change his mind. The salary would still not match up to what his new employers were offering but the option allowed him to continue doing what he knew he was good at and in a city that he loved. The decision was not easy and the fact that Rishi had been a friend and mentor to him only made it harder for Akash to take a contradictory stand. It took several discussions over the next few days before Rishi ruefully agreed to relieve him by the end of the month subject to his handover being complete by then.

Six days of the week, he had been immersed in handing over the various tasks that he was engaged in to another colleague who was to take over his role and on Sunday morning he was ringing the doorbell of Deepali's house. Deepali had told her parents about Akash and as expected, they were eager to meet him. Ideally, he would have liked to be prepared for such an encounter with some rehearsed lines and ready answers to the most likely questions that he was bound to face. His hectic schedule however, had denied him the luxury of prior preparation and he could now feel an anxious tremor in his knees.

"Come in *beta*," it was Deepali's mother, and he obviously was the guest of honor which meant that he was not required to give an introduction. He quietly followed her into the drawing room where a gargantuan structure lay sprawled on the sofa, sifting its gaze from the television screen to him, the intruder. *Thank god for small mercies. What a disaster it would have been if she were to look anything like her father?*

"*Namaste* uncle," he said, flashing his most charming smile. "Oh, you must be Deepali's friend. Come sit," he responded, making a valiant effort to adjust his massive frame and free some space on the sofa. *Yeah, and you would have been expecting Barack Obama to walk in instead of me, when the door-bell rang?* Not wanting to be the cause for any further discomfort, he opted to sit on the nearby armchair. The start was as cold as the inaugural function of the winter Olympics and when Deepali's mother excused herself to get some tea for him, the weightiness in the air made the interval between two ticks of the wall clock seem much longer than usual. It was the first time that Akash had found himself in such a situation and for the lack of anything better to do, he focused his attention on the television set. A cricket test match was on and India wasn't even one of the two teams competing.

"So, do you know why you are here?" he spoke after watching an uneventful over being bowled. *What a stupid question. I am sure it is his first time too.*

"Yes uncle," he meekly responded, holding his gape in anticipation of the next question and shifting it back to the television set when nothing followed. 'Don't speak unless you are spoken to,' he remembered the words of wisdom he had picked up from some Hollywood flick. Thankfully, Deepali soon made an appearance with a tray containing cups of tea and snack bowls with her mother in tow. He wasn't exactly expecting an animated hug but the almost inaudible 'hello' that she uttered before placing one of the cups in front of him was astounding. Mechanically, she placed a cup each in front of all living beings occupying the room before grabbing one of her own and taking refuge on the other arm chair.

By now her mother had skillfully managed to reclaim some of the obscured space on the sofa and had squeezed herself in a seating position. "So, who all are there in your family beta?" she started with a more logical set of questions and soon the chill in the room started to neutralize. It was much easier to strike a reasonable conversation with someone who, for starters did not have a stance of a rugby player gearing up to pounce on you. After about an hour, Akash had revealed most of the information about his family that was available in public domain and had also soaked in enough information about Deepali's family which her mother had enthusiastically offered. He wasn't sure how Deepali's cousin who was settled in Nairobi and had married an African girl had a bearing on his own marriage, but he had grasped everything like a student getting his first lectures of trigonometry.

It was decided that Akash would arrange a meeting between the two families and that would determine the future course of his relationship with Deepali. Her father had not contributed much to the discussions except for the few words of advice that sounded more like a threat to Akash. "I understand that both of you are responsible adults, but please don't give us a chance to rethink our stance before we meet your parents. Our society is still not open to girls spending time with boys before they get married and I suggest that the two of you respect our position and not meet behind our backs till we are able to reach a decision." The only trace of genuine happiness Akash had noticed on his face was when he had broken the news that he would be shifting to Mumbai in less than a fortnight.

Pit stop – Gurgaon (15th January '10)

Today was the day that the world would witness the longest solar eclipse in over a hundred years and the ostentatious galactic interplay could also be sighted from certain locations in the Indian subcontinent. The fiery, ardent sun god would be subjugated by the naturally flaccid moon, yet another instance establishing the transitory nature of power and authority, albeit for only a couple of hours.

At 31 years of age, Akash had no reasons to complain from all that life had bestowed upon him, or so it seemed. A loving wife, a DINK (double income no kids) household, which to some translated into an amiable financial standing, and most importantly – a soaring career. It had been a little over two years that Akash had shifted to Gurgaon with his current assignment. He was heading the Marketing Services vertical for a multinational organization, reporting directly to the head of Marketing. He was responsible for the company's communication, including PR (Public Relations), Advertising and Market Research. The role meant a leap for him not only in terms of the responsibilities but also monetarily and he was only glad to move back to the city he considered his own.

Deepali had stayed back in Mumbai, not willing to let go of the house that they had painstakingly built and her own career which was shaping up as satisfactorily as his. She was heading the Strategic Planning division for the Mumbai Branch of her Advertising Agency and since she had remained with the same organization for over six years, she had managed to establish herself as a valuable and critical resource. It was not easy to remain with a single organization in an industry marred with average work tenures of below a couple of years and Deepali too had to resist some tempting offers along the way. It was some deep rooted value and an anomalous sense of attachment with her work that ensured the precedence of loyalty over practicality in shaping her decisions.

Both Deepali and Akash were required to travel a fair bit in their respective roles and invariably they would plan their trips in a manner that they got to spend the weekend with each other. At times when an official trip didn't seem likely, either of them would plan a personal trip and pay the other a visit; ensuring that they spent minimum of one weekend together in a month. Over and above that, the numerous other communication mediums like e-mail, mobile phones etcetera ensured that they were as informed about each others life as they were when living under one roof. The decision for Akash to shift base had been a practical one and they had been open to amending the personal aspects of their life in accordance and taking remedial measures if so warranted. The going however, had been good so far, both of them having found a zone of comfort in the existing arrangement.

"Akash, boss would see you now," it was Tina, the CEO's secretary on the intercom. *So, here it is.* Akash picked up the planner and the Cross pen from his table and strolled out of his cabin towards the other end of the corridor which housed the larger cabins that were occupied by the department heads and the CEO.

"Hi Tina," he said as he walked past her, realizing that he had forgotten to wish her when she had called him a few minutes back. Looking up from her screen, she smiled, signaling for him to walk in to the CEO's cabin. *I am sure she knows all that is cooking inside and it is amazing how her expressions don't even betray a whiff.*

"Good afternoon Roopam, Good afternoon," he wished the CEO first followed by the other occupants of the room which included his boss Ashutosh and the IT (Information Technology) and HR (Human Resource) heads. *So the agenda is indeed serious. Anything that warrants such a quorum has to be important.*

"Hi Akash, come, please take a seat," Roopam responded, the smile which was an integral part of his normally congenial demeanor, currently absent. Akash complied, negotiating the ensuing silence by curiously glancing at others who were present in the room and were most certainly better informed about the agenda of the meeting than he was. They in turn seemed to be waiting for someone to take the lead and open the discussion. The awkward silence that ensued was finally broken by Ashutosh.

"This is about the data leakage incident."

The incident had appeared in the previous day's newspapers and since then had been the single most dominant topic of discussion during coffee and lunch breaks in the office. The cyber crime cell had arrested a middleman who was attempting to sell a compact disc containing confidential customer data to a decoy customer. The data belonged to their company and contained personal details of customers who had bought insurance products from them. The newspaper article had gone on to question the processes and integrity of the financial institutions and raised concerns on the measures that were being adopted by them to ensure safety of customer information.

The regulators had not yet reacted to the incident, but a reprimand could be expected anytime soon. Moreover, such incidents were certainly avoidable for an industry that had been badly impacted by the global recession over the past year and was now struggling to reclaim some of its lost ground. The memory span of the general public is known to be short and if they were lucky, the incident would only result in a temporary downslide in their sales numbers. However, if the data found its way to one of their competitors, many of whom were smalltime players with limited work ethics and would not hesitate in wooing the customers with a targeted ambush of special offerings, the repercussions could be devastating. Akash had immediately activated the entire PR machinery at his disposal for damage control and salvaging whatever could be salvaged.

Press releases were prepared and circulated to major publications, interviews were arranged for the investigating officer with the media where he categorically stated that investigation was underway and at the face of it the incident seemed to be the handiwork of one or more individuals employed by the company. The company's processes were given a clean chit and it was promised that within days the perpetrators would be brought to books. Ashutosh had been satisfied with the efforts and had complimented Akash, just the last evening.

While he waited for a more detailed explanation for the sudden summon, he could feel a strong sense of fear, slowly but steadily taking control of his being. This summon wasn't exactly sudden and he had a vague idea of what was to unfold, but a part of him continued to reassure him, exactly the way it had done when Vikram had called the last evening or when he had received an e-mail from Tina today morning asking him to keep his calendar free for a meeting with the CEO later in the day. *It is all shaping up exactly the way Vikram had said it would, but there is bound to be some mistake. Vikram must have been overreacting to some senseless gossip that he would have come across somewhere. The meeting surely has a totally different agenda and it will all be out in the open soon.* He had managed to ignore his conversation with Vikram, not as much as giving it a thought till today morning, when he got Tina's e-mail. *'Just a coincidence,'* he had told himself then.

"As you know, the access to such confidential customer information is limited to the senior managers, which limits the potential access points for this data. There are reasons for us to believe that the CD might have been copied from your laptop. Would you have any idea as to how this might have happened?" Ashutosh continued in an extremely diplomatic manner. A deadly weapon, whether concealed or out in the open, has the same effect on the target it is eventually used on. Akash's worst fears had come to life and he could feel a fissure in his soul, growing like a blot of ink on a cotton cloth threatening to tear him apart. "My laptop? There obviously has been a misunderstanding," he heard himself say.

"It is not a misunderstanding. We have gone through the available information more than once before deciding to speak to you. I have always maintained that you are one of the brightest members of our team and it was as much a shock for me as it is for you. So, if there is something that you can tell us, which might help us understand as to how this might have happened...," Roopam spoke, gently taking over the reigns of the discussion from Ashutosh.

"I am sure sir, there has been some mistake. The CD could not have been written on my laptop." Akash was regaining his voice as the gravity of the accusation that was leveled started to sink in. "You might have written the CD for some other purpose and left it unattended from where it might have fallen into wrong hands," Roopam continued oblivious to the words Akash had just spoken. "There are times when we all end up being a little careless, especially given the amount of work pressure we handle on a daily basis," Ashutosh contributed, making a feeble attempt to give Akash a reasonable platform to be able to change his stance; almost like a mother gently trying to steer her child away from a lie he had already spoken and was now committed to defend. "Ashutosh, I have never written a CD with such data. In fact it has been quite some time since I have even accessed the customer database," Akash replied, almost desperate to be believed.

"Akash, all the customer data resides on a separate system, where it is stored and updated on a regular basis. We use a separate interface to access any details from this central database to avoid any errors or data loss that might accidentally happen. For every access request, this interface records the terminal ID from where the request has originated and the data files that have been viewed. This record shows that the same files that have been written on the CD, were accessed through your system, and on that particular day, there had been no other access request for the same set of files," the IT Head, Smita, who had been a silent spectator till then, spoke for the first time. She had simplified the complex process of data storage and retrieval for the benefit of the technologically lesser qualified members in the gathering.

"But somebody could have accessed the data earlier and stored it on his system," Akash reasoned, attempting to hit upon a loophole in the logic that was being used to implicate him. "No, that is also not possible. The main database is updated in a batch run, once every 24 hours. For us this batch run happens between

10.30 and 11.30 pm every night and the data on the CD contains the last set of updates that would have happened the night before it was burnt. The CD contains the details for the customers who bought their policies a day before it was accessed and written, so the person who wrote the CD would have had to necessarily access the data after 11.30 pm the previous day and as I said, these set of files were only viewed on your system since then and time of the next data upload," she explained, dousing the faint flicker of hope that had emerged.

"But you did access the database on 16th November?" Roopam asked. By debating the manner in which the CD could have been written by someone else, Akash had virtually accepted that he had indeed accessed the database on the said day. He had inadvertently shattered his own 'first line of defense' and Roopam had shrewdly latched on to the opening.

"No sir, I haven't accessed the database in over a couple of months. I really don't know why or how the system is showing that the access request came from my laptop," Akash almost pleaded. "Akash, enough is enough. We are all mature adults sitting in this room and such feeble excuses are not going to work. Initially we thought that this might have happened out of carelessness, but your uncooperative attitude is not helping anybody. You have no idea about the implications this might have on your career and your life, so don't make this any harder for all of us." Roopam had derived his conclusion from the discussion and Akash knew that the battle was as good as lost.

"I understand the seriousness sir, but I really didn't do anything. Since the time I joined, I have only worked in the interest of the company and my performance has been recognized all along. You tell me, why would I do something so silly?"

"The facts are all in front of you, there is nothing left for me to say. If we don't reach a conclusion here, we will be forced to share the facts with the authorities and let them use it as a part of their own investigation. You know what that means. Don't you?"

"I understand sir, but you don't expect me to own up to something that I have no clue about, do you?" The discussion was heading nowhere and Akash could see the life he had meticulously built, come crashing down. This was certainly the end of his employment here and possibly anywhere in the corporate world. He was likely to be tried for fraud and if his current stream of luck was anything to go by, convicted too. How would his family react? His parents, who were always so proud of him, Deepali... would she understand? And more importantly, would she believe him? The eclipse was underway; one that the world was watching with amazement and another that was on the verge of claiming its victim within the confines of this room.

He felt like an explorer who had traded all his worldly riches for a ship and set out chasing his dream to discover the unknown, spilling sweat and blood, overcoming obstacles, fighting the beasts of the oceans and the wrath of nature with the objective of some day setting foot on the land of his dreams. And just when the elusive land was no longer amorphous that he falls prey to an unknown deadly disease that reduces his proud, upright being into a meek and feeble structure before eventually claiming his life. Maybe he was only meant to set his sight on the land of his dreams and never his foot.

Milestone – The Marital Knot (June '03 to November '03)

Mumbai, the city of dreams, the financial capital of India, the city that houses the second largest film industry in the world and now, the city that would be home to one Mister Akash Malhotra. The city presented a complete contrast to Delhi with its much spoken about narrow roads, dreadful traffic conditions and equally horrific living conditions. *'How can someone build an entire building with some 50-odd flats, without a single one of them having a balcony?'* Akash thought when he engaged himself in the utmost important task of finding an abode in the city, and a respectable one at that, considering his marital status was likely to change in the near future.

Over the past week Akash had been preoccupied with winding up traces of his existence from Delhi and preparing for a new life in a new city. He had met Deepali only twice since the meeting with her parents. "You did a great job. I am so proud of you," she had mentioned, expressing her pride with a peck on his cheek. After a brief analysis of her parents reactions post the meeting, a conclusion was drawn that if not thoroughly impressed by their daughter's suitor, they surely didn't have a reason to hate him. Surprisingly, there hadn't been much discussion about him after he had left except for her father's warning of not meeting him till a decision about their marriage was arrived at, being reiterated for her benefit. "I think they are waiting to meet up with your folks before taking a stand on the matter. So, when do you intend to speak to them?" There were some decisions to be taken.

"I don't know, but I guess it will have to be sometime soon." Realizing that Akash had not exactly drawn up a plan of action as yet and not wanting to pressurize him any further, she continued, "I heard that there is an opening in the Strategy Planning department of our Mumbai office. I intend to speak with Anurag about it. Wouldn't it be great if this works out? We would actually get to spend some quality time together," she said, with a naughty grin, in an attempt to lighten the mood. Akash was overwhelmed with emotion at her childlike attempt to put on the backburner, an issue that was of paramount importance to her. He reached out for her hair with one hand and gently stroking it, playfully replied, "Yes darling, it would be great, but what do you mean by 'some quality time together'? Am I giving you a hard time while we are here?" They were sitting in a coffee shop and this was as much public display of affection as they could permit themselves to engage in.

The same evening Akash called up home and spoke with his mother. His father was the more practical and understanding of the two and it would have been much easier to break the news to him, but mindful of the fact that he was depriving his mother of a fantasy that every Indian mother with a son nursed, the fantasy of being the one to carefully choose the girl who he would get married to, he decided to speak to her instead. If she was disappointed at having been deprived of the pleasure of finding a bride for her only son, it didn't show at all. She showered him with a flurry of questions, unable to contain her excitement. What is her name? What does she look like? Do you have a photograph of her? As the news slowly sunk in, the excitement started to settle and the questions became more probing. Who all are there in her family? What caste do they belong to? What does her father do?

He answered most of her questions rehearsing and rephrasing the words in his mind before speaking them out, just as any proficient lawyer would do while arguing a case in the courtroom. The idea in both cases being – to not leave an opening amidst the play of words which could be detrimental to the manner in which the case was meant to be presented. His mother continued to rally the information to his father, who Akash imagined to be sitting on the living room sofa, addressing him at times and otherwise relying on her own high pitch, in which she repeated some of the important points that Akash had said. "Oh, so they have a garments business and she is the only daughter?" Akash could imagine her holding the telephone line and looking at his father for any kind of a reaction in the affirmative or negative, but he knew that his father, though assimilating every bit of information being presented, would be focused on the television screen, not giving her any visual clue about his thoughts. In the end, his mother as always, summed up the conversation. "I will speak to your father and find out how soon we can come to Delhi and meet er…er.. Deepali? Such a pretty name, I can't wait to see what she looks like."

It was two days before he was to leave for Mumbai that his parents came to visit him. Akash had discussed their parents first meeting with Deepali at length and both of them had agreed upon a lunch meeting at a neutral venue, a reasonably upscale family restaurant in the Greater Kailash Market. While Akash preferred this arrangement since it would spare him the horror of facing 'Mr. Sumo' (a name that lacked in creativity but aptly described Deepali's father and one that he would muse about in private, scared of mentioning it in her presence) at his home turf. Deepali on the other hand was as nervous as any girl in her position was expected to be and didn't want to extend her ordeal for a minute longer than was necessary. A restaurant setting also ensured that she would not be required to walk in from the kitchen carrying snacks and tea into a room full of curiously delving eyes like a ramp model – a sight that had been embedded in the psyche of all Indian brides-to-be by numerous Hindi movies.

The meeting went off better than expected. 'Mr. Sumo' had a sociable side to him that he had managed to conceal in his earlier appearance. He shared funny stories about the kind of people who visited his wholesale garment store - from the fashion designer called Manmeet Vohra whose unisex name only added to the gender confusion created by his appearance, to the ever nagging Punjabi aunty and her upwardly mobile daughter, Pinky, who could never reach a mutual decision on what should be bought. His mother in turn had her own stories from the streets of Meerut, some of which, Akash suspected were infringing on the copyrights of an undisclosed source and had nothing to do with the city of Meerut or its inhabitants.

There were serious topics like Deepali's culinary skills and her amiable nature that crept up every now and then, diligently woven in the flow of conversation by her mother, keen to stick to the purpose of the meeting – showcasing Deepali. Akash was glad to see that the two families had bonded well enough for a first meeting and could tell by the look on his mother's face that Deepali had passed the litmus test. The lunch ended with the two families exchanging addresses and phone numbers and promising to keep in touch. His mother asked for Deepali's horoscope and in turn promised to send Akash's as soon as she reached Meerut. The ground had been laid and it was now for the adults to take charge and steer the matter to its conclusion.

"She is a very sweet girl. I am proud of your choice," his mother said pulling him down to plant a kiss on his forehead, once they returned home. There was no room for prosaic expressions of sentiments in his father's scheme of things but his excitement too was clearly visible. He was concerned about the arrangements that would be required to host a wedding away from home, "It is going to be an expensive affair here in Delhi, but then Bombay (Mumbai, the new name for the city, was yet to find flavor with most old world North Indians, including his father) would have been worse," he added.

The three of them sat for a while, discussing the marriage before his mother left to pack Akash's material belongings. He had tried to reason with her that the Packers and Movers, who were expected the next morning, were being paid to pack and transport his things to Mumbai, but the thought of depending on a bunch of strangers to do the job was something she could not digest. Just after midnight, when they decided to retire, she had most of his things neatly packed in cartons and bags and the ones that were remaining were neatly arranged. The next afternoon, Deepali had called expressing her desire to come to the airport to see him off, but Akash refused. His parents were also coming to the airport and he did not want his attention to be a latent bone of contention between the two parties at such a crucial juncture of his life.

The company guest house in Juhu was his first real stopover in the city. Akash was entitled to a 15 day stay within which he was expected to find a house to move in. He had given himself five days for the task, since the Packers and Movers had assured him that his consignment would be ready for delivery on the sixth day. A willing tenant, hundreds of to-let advertisements in the papers everyday, a decent budget – the equation seemed rather simple, till the time Akash actually embarked on the arduous assignment. "Sorry, the society does not permit us to rent the flat to bachelors," a standard response to most calls he made through the 'to-let' advertisements finally made him turn to the necessary evil called real estate agents or in simpler terminology - brokers.

The first few places he saw were either too tawdry to be called livable or had approach roads that would bring the most crowded of Old Delhi streets to shame. His office was in Santa Cruz West and a simple enquiry about the prevailing rentals in the area had been enough for him to realize that he would surely not be staying anywhere close to his workplace. His search for a decent flat at an affordable price continued to lead him in the north-easterly direction till on the fourth day he finally stumbled across a one bedroom flat in the Sher-e-Punjab area of Andheri East.

The flat was on the sixth floor of an eight year old building and belonged to a business family living in the same locality. The building seemed slightly worn out for its age but was approachable, was within budget and most importantly the flat owner was able to look at bachelorhood as a phase of life rather than a condition that warranted the infected to be locked up in an asylum to prevent any further degradation of the society's moral values. Thus, Akash moved into the flat that would serve as his house for the first couple of years of his married life.

Akash's role as an Assistant Brand Manager for one of the detergent brands of his company was very different from his earlier assignment. In addition to brand communication, he was also responsible for analysis of the sales trends, market share data and formulating the overall brand strategy. Although he was vaguely familiar with these terms, he was looking forward to the learning experience and once he had settled into his new house, he took to his work with a renewed vengeance. Seven day weeks and late hours in the office became a norm and the fact that he knew virtually no one in the city other than the few friends he had made at work, made things much easier. He was used to staying away from his parents but there were times that he would miss Deepali's company.

They would talk for hours every night, narrating every small incident that had occurred during the day, sharing their deepest emotions and planning the things they would do once they were together. As soon as Akash would sit in the auto to head home, his longing for hearing her voice would take charge and he would curse the traffic that had to be countered before the seclusion and privacy of his bedroom allowed him to make the call that served as a lifeline for him in this alien city.

The hustle-bustle and the fast paced life that Mumbai is known for, continued unabated. For Akash it was like a jaunt to Necropolis (The ancient 'city of the dead'). Heedless of the life around him, he went about leading his own in a manner that treaded on the thin line between focus and melancholy. A part of him, it seemed, had been left behind and he was attempting to fill the void by immersing himself in more and more work. His efforts had helped his performance but his colleagues after a few feeble attempts at socializing, had written him off as a loner who had no life beyond the confines of his cubicle in office. When they went about exploring the latest hang-outs in the city on Saturday nights, Akash would be lost in Deepali's thoughts and would be eager to head back home and speak to her.

It had been about four months since he had shifted to Mumbai and as usual, he was buried in a series of Gant Charts and Excel Sheets when a pop-up indicated the arrival of a new e-mail message. It was Deepali. Since, the regular e-mail sites were blocked on his office network, they had resorted to dropping a line on each others official IDs when something important needed to be shared. He hurriedly clicked on the message which read, "I am coming to Mumbai… ye, ye, ye… Call when you can... I am so excited... Kiss." Akash could hardly believe his eyes. Just to ensure that words had not played a trick on him, he read the message once again before picking up his mobile phone and heading out to the privacy of one of the conference rooms to call her.

"Remember... I had told you about this opening in our Mumbai office?" she started, in her usual calm manner. "They have given you that role?" he cut her short, unable to contain his excitement. "Hold your horses darling," she said in an almost teasing tone, "Yes, I think I have got the job." "Wow, that's superb. So, when do they want you to join?"

"Actually, Anurag had just called me to say that he had shared my profile with the Mumbai branch head sometime back and he had just received an e-mail from him saying that they were fine with looking at me for the role. He wants to have a telecon with me before finalizing the details, but Anurag says that the call is just a formality and I should get the job." For the rest of the day, Akash was a totally different person in office, smiling at people, laughing heartily over jokes cracked by his colleagues, that he otherwise would have missed even taking note of. "Which side of the bed did you get up from, today? You know you should make it your regular side," Sudipta, one of his colleagues remarked on his sudden transformation.

The same evening Deepali called him back with the good news. The telecon had happened and she had formally been offered the role. The Mumbai Branch wanted her to join as soon as possible but since Anurag needed time to find a replacement for her, the joining date had been fixed for two months from now. Akash was elated and was dying to share the news with his mother. He left office early and as soon as he sat in the auto rickshaw, he dialed his home number on the mobile – the privacy of his bedroom was not really required when he was speaking to his mother.

"That is great news! But how will the marriage happen in such a short time?" Her son, in a far away land, with a girl he was romantically inclined towards, was a thought she obviously could not digest, even if the girl was her daughter-in-law to be. This statement suddenly brought back memories of Mr. Sumo's parting statement to him during their first meeting - "You are both responsible adults… I suggest that the two of you don't meet behind our backs." The news was sure to catch him by surprise and Akash couldn't have been more accurate with his judgment. Within half an hour of the conversation with his mother, he got a call from Deepali who had reached home by now and broken the news to her parents.

"Papa says that we must get married before I shift to Mumbai. I really don't know what to do," she said with a tinge of despair. The misery of having managed to resolve one big problem, only to discover a bigger one staring her in the face, was evident in her voice. Akash had the advantage of having gone through the same thoughts a little while earlier and by now had thought through the potential answer to this new problem. "My mother was saying the same thing, but then what is the problem? I know it is a little tight, but why can't we get married within the next two months?"

The two households immediately got into hyperactive mode with frantic activity to make the required arrangements for the marriage. Akash got regular telephonic updates of the developments on both sides through his mother and Deepali. The *Pundit* had been summoned to decide on an auspicious date with clear instructions that it needed to be as late as possible, as long as it was within the next two months. It is strange how the right amount of *Dakshina* can help you negotiate your terms even with the deities. "27th November– the date of our marriage leaves us with no time for the honeymoon, but I am not complaining." Deepali had informed him. She had to join her new office in Mumbai on the 1st of December.

Amidst the flurry of activity and excitement, Akash had managed to recover his lost self back. Though his focus on work did not subside, he suddenly managed time to join his colleagues for their after office outings and engage in frivolous banter during lunch and tea breaks. It was as if a coconut had shred its shell to expose its white and creamy side to the world. "I never thought we would be friends. God only knows how you managed to behave like a 20 something, grumpy old man all this while," Sudipta continued to tease him about his near reincarnation at every possible opportunity. His new friends were happy to hear about his marriage and had promised to attend his wedding in Delhi. Some of them had even started quizzing him on the amount of woolen clothes they would require to be able to return alive from the dreaded Delhi winters.

Deepali had recently introduced him to a social networking site that was not blocked on his office network. This enabled them to keep in touch with each other on a continuous basis without using their official e-mail IDs. They could write general comments on each others profiles, send private messages and update whatever they were doing on their profile 'status'. Akash had the site continuously open on his screen and he knew that Deepali would also be tracking everything he wrote on a real time basis. This virtual connection could not be compared with being in the physical company of the one we love, but it was a close second.

Since he was still new in his current job, Akash had taken leave only from the 24th to the 30th of November, leaving most of the pre-marital arrangements under the able supervision of his parents. As the time of his departure to Delhi neared, the wait seemed even longer. He was anxiously waiting for one of the happiest moments of his life but time would simply prohibit him from flying off to it. In Metaphysics, Aristotle defines time in terms of the 'moment' or 'now'. This 'now', akin to the atom is indivisible and time is the line that joins these individual 'nows' or 'moments'. Time is the universal order within which all changes are related to each other and all finite things are necessarily a part of it.

Akash's finite wait had his own set of moments woven together by the thread of time. Getting the courier containing his wedding invites and posting them to his friends, shopping for the *Sherwani* he would wear on the big day and simply thinking about Deepali and himself - together on the raised platform accepting wishes and presents made the 'moments' numerous. Though Akash was relishing every one of them, he was eager for their passage so as to permit the 'ultimate moment' to arrive and so it did.

His parents had rented a 3 bedroom flat, which served as the base camp for the groom side of the marriage contingent. The gathering wasn't particularly large since the ticket fare to Delhi (which the attendees were expected to bear themselves) proved a deterrent for most freeloaders, allowing only for the immediate family and friends to be present for the occasion. The marriage ceremony was arranged in one of the banquet halls of a four star hotel in South Delhi. Deepali's parents had not left any stone unturned to ensure that the marriage scaled all heights of grandeur that their finances permitted. The floral decoration predominantly comprising of white lilies, the lavish dinner spread and a live DJ made the event a memorable one. But the one memory that Akash would always remember the day by, was that of Deepali taking measured steps towards the stage in a metallic orange *Lehngha* looking down at the carpet ahead of her, being escorted by her cousins – a graceful walk from one life to another; a walk that comes ever so naturally to every bride at the time of her wedding.

The *mahurat* was late in the night and by the time the rituals were all accounted for, it was 5.00 am. A suite had been booked for the newly weds in the same hotel – the honeymoon suite, a room where numerous lovers had discovered the ultimate pleasures of life before retiring in the arms of their beloved. But Deepali's conniving hairdresser had her own evil designs. Once within the confines of the honeymoon suite, Deepali turned to Akash for help in removing the pins that had been used to create an amalgamated bundle with her natural hair and a cosmetic extension. Eager to help, he walked into the trap, unmindful of what lay in store as the count of successfully extracted pins kept mounting. Each layer of pins successfully removed gave way to a new concealed one, carefully stuck inside. After about 20 minutes and 76 pins, Akash was too exhausted even to breathe and Deepali's state would have been no different, for when he got up the next afternoon, she was still sleeping on his side, wearing her bridal *Lehngha.*

The next two days were packed with post marriage rituals, meeting out of station relatives before they left and various financial settlements. Finally on the morning of 30th November, Mr. and Mrs. Malhotra boarded their flight to Mumbai, embarking on a new journey of life.

Acclimatization – Mumbai (December '03 to December '04)

Upon her arrival in Mumbai, the first thing Deepali did was to take charge of the house that Akash, in his own right, had prepared for her arrival. Over the next few days, Akash came to terms with facts which had surprisingly eluded him during his bachelorhood days. He realized that the washing machine did not object to washing pairs of socks that had been worn for just a day. It was as easy, perhaps easier, to locate a pair of shoes that had been placed in the shoe rack the previous evening as against when they were left to fend for themselves on the bedroom floor. A cup of tea could also be made with just the right proportion of milk and sugar and this need not necessarily be a fluke. A button falling off a shirt did not always mean that the shirt had outlived its prescribed existence. These and many more such revelations marked Akash's initiation into married life and with each revelation he found his fondness for Deepali growing.

"Could you manage to pick up the packet of flour I had asked you to?" she would ask with a frown on her face, mindful of the fact that Akash would have forgotten all about the request she had made the previous evening. "Oh! Actually, I was thinking that we should order food from *Shiv Sagar* today. Office must have been tiring for you as well and once in a while you should take a break from your cooking," he would try to recoup. "Really? Well, thanks for the concern, but there is no need to order food. I picked up the flour on my way back and dinner is almost ready," she would state before storming off to the kitchen. Akash would make feeble promises with the most gullible expression he could muster and soon her playful annoyance would vanish and dinner would be served amidst a repartee known only to the newly-weds. They would discuss any and everything from incidents in office to page three gossip and would never be short of things to share with each other. Eventually they would retire to their bedroom, the ensuing darkness conjuring a scene of unbridled passion resulting out of the boundless craving they felt for each other.

It is often heard, that the true colors of otherwise seemingly compatible couples, are uncloaked when left to adjust with each other under the confines of a single roof. For Akash and Deepali, this concept seemed to be working in the reverse. Whether this was due to the fact that this alliance had evolved from a platform of friendship and understanding or due to some incomprehensible cosmic interplay, both of them were enjoying every bit of their world's profundity, its unbounded beauty.

In Deepali's company, Akash was rediscovering not only facets of his personality that he thought had faded away with time, but also numerous aspects of the city that had remained veiled from him. Like most Delhi'ites, the world of television and cinema had remained a mystifying fascination for her and she would leap with excitement at the mere sight of any remotely recognizable face from this world. "Look. Look. The girl in the green top… over there. Isn't she the one who plays *Astha* in that serial on Zee TV?" she would whisper, attempting to be discreet but mostly unable to contain her excitement. "May be," Akash would casually remark, not meaning to disappoint her with his limited expertise in the matter. The excitement would continue till such time that she would call her mother and a few other friends in Delhi, giving them a word by word narration of the rare sighting. "She looks so different off screen, just like a normal girl," he would hear her animated description, at times wondering how she would react if ever she came face to face with one of the Bollywood biggies, an occurrence that wasn't particularly atypical to the city.

Her excitement served as an immense source of pleasure for Akash and he would make an effort to take her to places that the cinema folk were known to frequent. From having coffee at the Lotus Café in the J W Marriot hotel to watching a movie at Cinemax, Versova, he would plan most of their weekend outings with the ulterior motive of coming across anyone recognizable enough to propel her into an exhilarating frenzy. The circuitous delight derived from bringing joy to our loved ones, far supersedes any that can be derived through self indulgence. The quintessential mother from Hindi movies who goes to lengths to ensure that her offspring does not sleep hungry; the innocent child who competes ferociously in the school sports day to witness the pride on his parents face; and Akash Malhotra finding bliss in doing little things to make Deepali happy, were all a testimony to this fact.

Though not exactly a theatre connoisseur, Akash had once got tickets for a play starring the yesteryear star Shabana Azmi. Deepali had sat dumbfounded for the entire hour and half unable to believe that she was sitting barely a few meters away from the actor watching her perform live. After the show ended,

Akash requested Ms Azmi for a photograph with Deepali and she gladly obliged. This photograph had been the topic of conversation in their household for days to come and had been uploaded on all the social networking sites where Deepali had an account. "You remember Kiran? The friend from college I had told you about? She commented on the photo with Shabana on Facebook today. I am so happy, I love you so much," she would say before giving him a tight hug. *Thank you Shabana. I am sure you would have had an impact on the lives of many married men, but of this nature, I am sure mine is the first.*

Deepali had taken to the city like a house on fire. She enjoyed the hustle-bustle of the streets, the tranquility of staring for long hours into the incessant ocean from the sea side café in Juhu, the boisterous night life and the privacy of their home. "This city allows you to lead your life the way you want to. People are non-interfering and believe in minding their own business. And most importantly, it is so much safer for women here." Mumbai sure was a very different city from Delhi – much more tolerant, professional and yes, safe for women. It was commonplace to find girls window shopping in the Lokhandwala Market, wearing clothes that would have called for the implementation of marshal law on the streets of Delhi. Deepali would call it the "cosmopolitan culture" while Akash thought it was another Indian attempt to ape the west and a fairly successful one at that. Certain pockets of the city exuded a charm akin to any of the big western cities. Had one Mr. Joseph Rudyard Kipling been in Mumbai in the current times he would certainly have to rethink his oft-quoted lines – '*Oh, East is East and West is West and never the twain shall meet.*'

The influence of the city was also evident in Deepali's wardrobe, which in addition to her trademark Punjabi suits, now comprised of numerous pairs of trousers, peddle pushers, skirts and tops. At times when she would get ready for their Friday night 'partying out', Akash would be stunned at the metamorphosis she would undergo within a span of a few minutes. Short, hip hugging skirts that revealed her waxed legs way above the knee, worn with carefully chosen tops which did justice to her voluptuous bust line while refraining from revealing the slight deposit of fat on her sides in cahoots with the slight make-up, would transform her into an even more desirable entity. Initially, Akash was wary of the few milliseconds of additional attention she would draw from the prying male eyes, but he eventually got accustomed to it. Her attire was perfectly normal, in fact a little bit on the conservative side, in comparison with the 'bare all' dresses that he would see other girls adorning. Invariably, his mounting desire for her through such evenings would culminate into a passionate and hungry session of love making when they returned home in the wee hours of the morning.

'He who loves lives, he who is selfish is dying,' Akash and Deepali were following Swami Vivekananda's first of the fifteen laws of life to the hilt. A pair deeply immersed in love, cruising through life on a high tide. Time continued its journey, piercing together their exquisite moments into a year full of charming memories. Love they say has a bearing on all that comes in its proximity. Strange as it may sound, but a scientific study, if conducted, would certainly have thrown up a strong correlation between the love in Akash's life and the sale of detergents in the country, especially the brand that Akash managed. The market share of his brand had been steadily rising over the past few quarters and was now sitting at a healthy 26% in a market crammed with various national and international players. Some of the trade promotions that he had conceptualized had worked wonders and one of them had even been presented at the Asia Pacific level by the India Management Team during their annual review – an extremely rare privilege for anyone at his level.

Deepali's joie de vivre was palpable and with time it had managed to seep into Akash's being. He had this strange sense of contentment about him which instead of deterring his ambitions, enabled him to go about them in an extremely calm and composed fashion. He had long, shred the tag of being a loner, which had been unwillingly attached to him during his first few months in the city, a side effect of being in a long distance relationship. Things however were no longer the same now and most people in the office had grown to like his company. This, coupled with his zeal to excel at work, had made him into a definite recipe for success in the corporate set-up.

"Your performance during the last year has been exceptionally good. Just continue what you have been doing and I am sure that a bright and rewarding career awaits you in the years to come," Prasad, his boss had told him during his mid-year appraisal. Prasad was an intelligent fellow and an aggressive professional in an extremely timid sort of a way. The plastic rimmed spectacles, well oiled hair and diminutive structure all contributed to the inconsequential appearance – an appearance as deceiving as could be. Prasad was ruthless when it came to execution and almost obsessive about getting things done in the right manner and on time. He knew his numbers like the back of his hand, which enabled him to have an objective view about everything. He could tear apart a well thought through proposal within a matter of seconds, which meant that everything that passed through his table had to be thoroughly assessed and re-assessed beforehand.

Working with Prasad had been a tremendous learning experience for Akash. Though it had taken some time but in due course he had succeeded in proving his reliability and winning Prasad's confidence. Akash brought to the table the one ingredient that his boss had not been amply bestowed with – a creative mind. Prasad covertly acknowledged this fact by turning to Akash in times of creative ideation, giving adequate regard to his thoughts and suggestions. Their individual skill sets fit together like pieces of a jigsaw puzzle making them a formidable team. Though they did not share much of an informal rapport, a strong sense of mutual respect defined their relationship. Akash admired Prasad for his knowledge, looked up to him as a mentor and respected him as a nice human being, albeit masked behind a tough exterior. It was the kind of relationship Akash shared with his boss that was responsible for his mixed reactions to the news, when he was faced with it.

He had just come back from a trip to Kashid, a quaint seaside village at a few hours drive from Mumbai. "So Mr. Malhotra, how does it feel to be married for exactly a year now?" Deepali had asked him with her usual luminous smile and a mischievous grin that he could not quite comprehend at that moment. Akash had left office early that evening and ventured out to the Bandra Linking Road market to pick up Deepali's first anniversary gift. It had to be something special, something that could level up to the occasion. Over the past few days Akash had thought of numerous items ranging from the latest mobile handset to a solitaire ring but none of these came remotely close to the sentiments he wanted his first anniversary gift to express. It was Sudipta who came to his aid and helped him overcome his dilemma. Taking her advice, he contacted a portrait artist and e-mailed him a few of their wedding photographs. The Friday evening traffic was maddening but he managed to reach home by his usual time after picking up the portrait and a black forest cake, a surprise gift for Deepali. He had left both the items with a neighbor for safekeeping before entering the house.

"We still have a few hours to go before we complete one full year," he said, casually glancing at the clock, "but it has been all that I dreamt of and more." The usually non emotive Akash could feel an uncontainable surge emerging out of the enormity of the moment. "Awww... My baby," planting herself on his lap she draped her arm around his neck, pulling him closer till they could feel the collision of each others breath. *There goes dinner. But to hell with it.* Akash tightened his grip on her waist, rubbing his face on her dense black hair looking for an opening to bury himself in the curve joining her neck to the rest of her body.

At exactly 11.50, he picked up his mobile phone and casually walked out of the main door. "Let me call my mother. She would be awake waiting to wish us," he said, pulling the door behind him. He waited for a few seconds before planting the phone back in his pocket and gently walking to the other end of the lobby to press the neighbor's doorbell. Deepali was ecstatic. As the intricately carved frame of the portrait gleamed in her hand, she kept looking at their lifelike images staring back at her from the most important day of their lives, the day they got married, till a soundless trickle emerged from her moist eyes. "I love you. I love you more than anything in this world," she said, finally shifting her sight to the real Akash. He had heard these words from her repeatedly over the past year, almost habitually, but today they seemed to be carrying a completely different meaning. Akash was overwhelmed too. As he lay on the bed, Deepali curled up against him; he couldn't help but feel a sense of pride for being able to make this day a special one for her. He also felt a fleeting tinge of disappointment which he quickly overcame. *She didn't get me anything for our anniversary? Was it possible that she had forgotten about it?*

"Get up lazy bones, we don't have much time," Deepali was sitting on the bedside, gently stroking his hair. "But why in God's name? It is Saturday and we are in no hurry to get to work," he said, trying to pull her closer. "No," she firmly said, pushing his hand away. "Get up and get ready. Don't ask questions, just do as I say." Akash was puzzled, but the determination in her voice left no scope for bargaining. Grumpily he pulled himself out of the bed and headed for the washroom. When he finally emerged, he saw Deepali had already laid out his clothes on the bed and was busy packing something into a small bag. "Are we going somewhere?" "No questions, I said," she retorted, without looking up towards him. As he carried the bag to the lift, he knew that she had planned something. *But what is it. And what is with this bag? Where are we going?*

A private taxi was waiting for them near the building gate and apparently the driver had received his instructions beforehand. There was no dialogue and as soon as they took their seat, he put the vehicle in motion and so it remained for the next three hours. Akash tried to guess their destination a couple of times, aided by the road signs but Deepali simply refused to react. It was only when they reached the Prakruti Beach Resort in Kashid that the mystery unraveled itself. Deepali had gone at great lengths to plan this weekend trip. Their cottage was on one end of the resort, almost isolated, with the backdoor opening into a veranda overlooking the beach. Within moments of reaching the room, Deepali pulled out a bottle of red wine and cheese cubes from somewhere. "Happy anniversary my darling," she said, looking at him while slowly drilling the cork screw into the bottle.

They sat in the veranda, sipping on the wine and staring into the ocean, intermittently stealing a glance at each other. There were no words spoken and yet the silence continued to abet an exchange – an abstract exchange that even thousands of words could not accomplish. *This is life. And it is so beautiful. She is so beautiful. Oh, how I love her.* When the first bottle got over, Deepali miraculously produced another one and then yet another, till they drifted away from the world around them to the comfort of their own world, a world with only two inhabitants.

The next two days were heavenly and by the end of it Akash was convinced that they had not had enough of the place and couldn't return just as yet. Dining amidst the melody of live Ghazals, lying down on the beach looking at the thousands of twinkling stars and trying to make sense out of the arbitrary shapes they conjured, walking into the clear blue waters holding hands, all of it was not meant to end so soon. "I think I can manage a couple of days of leave. I can text my boss and check. Anyway, there isn't much work in office now-a-days, plus I haven't taken any leave since the time I have shifted here," she said, looking at him expectantly. The ball was in his court now. Akash also called up Prasad to check if he could join work on Wednesday. "Oh, so you finally managed time for your honeymoon?" he cracked one of his rare jokes. "It is fine. I will hold fort, but you will surely be able to join office on Wednesday, right?"

"Yes Prasad, of course. I will be in office on Wednesday morning. Thank you so much."

On Wednesday morning, as Akash ambled through the office entrance, making his way to the lift, he tried hard to remember the pressing issues he had left behind while leaving office the last Friday. The holiday, though brief, had made him loose all sense of time and obligation, a wonderful hiatus minus the vagaries of his usual day to day life. He felt like a child returning to school after a long summer break, dreading the thought of being re-saddled with the burdens he knew were fated. As he reached his work station, pausing to recall his password, he was glad to have come in early since this would give him some time to settle before the days action actually began. There were a few people from other departments he could see on the floor, but no one that he felt obliged to walk up and greet.

Sudipta was the first person to walk up to him, "So dude, how was it? I tried to call you but your number was not reachable," she said, crossing her hands over her chest and leaning against his desk. "Oh, it was fabulous. Deepali had planned a surprise outing to Kashid and maybe that's why you could not get through to me. The signals there were pretty erratic."

"I have heard so much about that place. It must have been fun? Prasad had mentioned that you had gone out of town but not the exact location. By the way…," she stopped halfway through the sentence looking over Akash's shoulder, "Good morning Prasad," she added. "Good morning Sudipta. Hi Akash, welcome back. And before you get caught up with other pressing issues, can we chat up for a bit?" he said signaling towards one of the vacant conference rooms. Prasad wasn't particularly known for his social ways but Akash was expecting him to enquire about the vacation or at least wish him. Surprised at the starched conduct, he followed Prasad to the conference room. *What was Sudipta's thumb up gesture supposed to mean? And what was it that she was trying to say before Prasad appeared on the scene?*

"I don't know if you have heard this, but on Monday some organizational changes were announced. And one of them includes my movement to Singapore in a regional marketing role," Prasad spoke as a matter of fact. "Wow, that's fantastic. Many congratulations," was his immediate reaction. "Hold on my dear. There is more to come," Prasad said, a hint of a smile managing to appear on his lips for the first time since the morning. "I am required to move into my new role by Christmas which hardly leaves us with any time here. There were lots of discussions on my replacement but in the end everyone agreed that in your short stint with the organization, you have managed to demonstrate enough commitment and ability to take on the role. We were waiting to have a word with you before the decision was made public. So, do you think you are up for it?" Akash was in state of shock and Prasad's smile was now a full fledged one, exhibiting most of his pale white teeth.

Is this some kind of a joke? No, but Prasad is not the kinds to fool around. Akash was speechless, not knowing how to react to this completely unexpected news. All he managed to utter was, "Yes, I suppose." "Very well then, I shall have a word with HR and ask them to release the official communication soon," he said, extending his hand for a shake. "Thank you Prasad." "It is time to celebrate my boy and not look as if someone has stolen a prized possession off you. We shall discuss this at length later, after I set the ball rolling," Prasad said, leaving Akash to cherish his moment of joy. He slumped back into the chair, staring into oblivion, trying to get a grip on the array of thoughts that had suddenly started to emerge from all nook and corners of his mind. *Wow. This is really happening. I hope I am able to manage without Prasad. Will this only be a role change or also entail a promotion and possibly a salary hike? Will I get someone reporting in to me? Deepali would be ecstatic.*

Sudipta was the first one to bump into him again as he emerged from the conference room, whether by coincidence or design, he would never know. "So, you got it, right?" she asked with a knowing smile. Akash nodded. "The minute I heard about Prasad's move, I knew that you would be the one replacing him. Congratulations dude, you deserve it," he was touched by the genuine thrill and excitement in her voice. Akash was over elated and as is the case with most, his heightened state of emotions had cornered him to an extremely fragile state of mind. He needed an outlay, someone who could help him contain the sparks of sentiments that were oozing from within. "Thank you. I am glad, I managed not to disappoint you," he casually patted her on the shoulder, reaching out for his phone to break the news to Deepali.

He got the answers to most of his questions over the next few days. Akash would take over from Prasad as the Brand Manager for the detergent business which comprised of two brands – one, the company's flagship brand and the other, a recently acquired regional brand having a strong presence in a few of the southern states. He would have an Assistant Manager reporting into him, a candidate he would have to recruit soon. The elevation in rank had also been accompanied by a handsome pay hike; a tangible reward for his efforts that had an amplifying effect on Deepali's already magnified reactions to the news.

She had coaxed Akash into inviting his entire team home to celebrate the promotion and also to bid farewell to Prasad. Akash would have preferred taking the team out for dinner but since most of the efforts involved in inviting them home were to be Deepali's, he had given in after a timid protest. The get together had turned out to be an interesting affair with Prasad having a drink too many. This was the first time that Akash had seen him nearly drunk and his farewell speech in the same inebriated state had been an amusing experience for the rest of the audience.

Deepali had played a perfect host ensuring that she spoke and mingled with everyone in attendance. The only invitee conspicuous with her absence was Sudipta, but except for the few mentions of her not having turned up, not many people seemed to have missed her. Later when the guests left, Akash remained awake on his bed, an exhausted Deepali clinging to him, dreaming of the great times that lay ahead. Let Monsignor Time do his tedious, devious work and he shall serve you on a platter all that you deserve and more.

Acceleration – Life In A Fast Lane (December '04 to May '06)

"I am going to Bangalore on Friday. There are a series of client presentations scheduled over Friday and Saturday and I am expecting to be back only by Sunday morning," Deepali informed Akash. In line with the corporate world norms where every ambitious individual was expected to put in that little bit extra to make them shine over the others, once in a while either of them found themselves spending a part of their weekend at work. Whenever this happened, Akash would be furious. He often quoted the example of western nations where people struck a balance between their work and personal lives and no one expected others to work over weekends. "It is our inefficiency mostly, and at times the convoluted logic of trying to impress the boss which is responsible for our plight," he would say. Weekends and holidays were not meant for work, this was their time, time that they should be spending in each others company doing things that their hearts desired.

Although he had strong views on the subject, he wasn't exactly prepared to become a martyr for the cause and would be found dragging himself to work when the situation so demanded. He would be as cantankerous when he returned home as he would have been while leaving for work. This crankiness would multiply manifold when the one to give in to the nefarious demands of the workplace would be Deepali and he would be left to negotiate his disappointment in the company of no one but himself. However, today was different. He did not feel any fumes emerging within him from the irritation that such situations were known to cause. Instead he was indifferent. In fact a part of him was glad that he would get some time of his own, a fact that he avoided acknowledging even to himself.

An increase in responsibility had its own pitfalls and he found himself spending more time in the office than earlier. His new boss, Shantanu, the Brand Head was a forty something divorcee who found solace from life in the office and seemed to be engaged in constant machinations to keep his team members grasping for breath under the burden of work. A Management Trainee, fresh out of Business School had been inducted into the team and was helping Akash in managing his brands. Her being inexperienced meant that Akash had to review and supervise everything she did. This, in addition to his own regular work translated into more time being spent at his desk and he had been returning home well past midnight for a better part of the past couple of months.

During his lucky weekends, when he would manage to keep himself out of office, Deepali and Akash would follow their usual routine. Going to a night club on Saturday evening, shopping for the next week's ration on Sunday morning, watching a movie, hair cut, parlor visit, washing of clothes, a broken tap or a faulty electrical appliance that needed to be fixed, the occasional visits to the bank, Deepali invariably had an airtight schedule ready before the weekend began. Though all the tasks were either necessities or of recreational nature, by the end of it Akash found that he was as exhausted as he had been when the weekend started. The very thought of not having to get out of bed till as long as he wished and following a timetable that had nothing on it, was something that he was looking forward to.

On Thursday night, Deepali packed an overnighter and as per plan, left for the airport early the next morning. Akash was asleep when she left. Her goodbye came in the form of a text message which he got on the way to his office. "Have boarded. Flight is 20 mins late. You take care and see you on Sunday. Kiss," it read. Akash replied with a "You take care too…," but the message went undelivered. *She would have switched off her phone.* Deepali had managed to strike a good balance between her professional and personal life. She continued to return home before Akash and cook for them; she would attend to various nuances of running a household – from ordering a refill of the cooking gas cylinder to paying the electricity bills, tasks that would remain pending for weeks if left to Akash. Amidst all this she masterfully created time for leisure and merriment, probably a result of her exuberance and insatiable thirst for life.

Though, unlike Akash she would never whine about the frantic pace that life demanded of her to keep up with it, the frenzy was surely taking a toll on her. Her childlike antics and playfulness had subsided and would now surface only in erratic bursts. The little kid of their bi-habited world had matured over the last couple of years and now there was rarely a difference between the Deepali of their world and the Deepali that the outside world had known all along. It seemed as if she had subconsciously restrained herself and the fissure to her nucleus that was earlier open to Akash was slowly healing. She, who would never pass a chance to plant a kiss on his cheek and express her undying love, now seemed much more contained and reserved. In fact it had been a while that Akash had heard from her the three magical words that form the core of many a relationships, "I love you."

The Saturday without Deepali was progressing as he had hoped – uneventful and lazy, with no immediate compulsions that required him to get out of the bed. As Akash flipped through the newspaper, his thoughts continued to take an introspective form making him look back at the two years of married life they had completed. *What had changed? Had anything changed at all or was it simply a figment of his imagination – the convoluted intrigues of a tired mind? Had he changed? Or, was it Deepali who had changed?*

He recalled a recent incident when they had come face to face with a young Bollywood director who had become a sensation after delivering three back to back hits in a span of two years, at a shopping mall. "Hey, aren't they Adarsh Kashyap and his Russian girlfriend? She is looking so pretty in a salwar suit and she is also taller than him," a glimpse of the celluloid smitten Deepali had flickered for a moment before being subdued by her current, mature persona. Later, on their way back home, she had called her mother and narrated the sighting – as enthusiastically as she had been doing since her advent to Mumbai. *No, she hadn't changed. She was still the same person.*

Her conduct with everyone in her life was the same as it would have been a couple of years back – but for him. Her mother for instance would know that she was as excited to see Adarsh as she had been when she had met Shabana Azmi. The only difference being that unlike Shabana, Adarsh would not be discussed for days within their household - in fact he would be lucky to earn a mention from Deepali once they got out of the car. Was it that their relationship that had lost some of its fizz and settled down after the initial whirlwind, like the sands of time? Was her excitement a ploy to keep concealed from her mother something of dire proportions that was brewing within her?

He checked his thoughts from drifting further into the restricted and frightfully dark zones that could sow seeds of cynicism in his mind. *I am making a mountain out of a mole hill – a classic example of an empty mind being the devil's workshop.* Deepali loved him and cared for him more than possibly anyone else in his life. She was a friend he could turn to at all times; someone who would stick by his side, irrespective of the circumstances. She was the only person ever to have understood him completely, accepting his strengths and weaknesses all in the same stride. Their bond existed in a plane, way beyond the reach of these trivialities. *I am being stupid. It is a simple case of monotony and work pressure momentarily impacting our lives and a little conscious effort is all that is required to get things back to where they should be.*

Akash, was not one to poke the ashes, for them to rise and pretend that the fire was never there. Something was changing in his life and though he could not put a finger to it, he knew that it was time to take control and bring things back to where they belonged. As he drove towards the airport to receive Deepali, a first in their two years of marriage, he stumbled across another possible reason for the continual loss of luster from their lives. *Have we started taking each other for granted? Why do I never offer to drop her to the airport or pick her up when she is traveling? Yes, booking a Cab is more convenient, but convenience is not what is supposed to dictate one's actions in a relationship. Is it?*

On Sunday mornings, the streets of Mumbai offer a delightful driving experience, free of the customary hustle-bustle and the sea of otherwise swarming vehicles. It took him ten minutes to reach the car parking in the 'Arrivals' area of the domestic airport. *What a sham, 100 rupees for parking a car for twenty minutes? Surely, hailing a cab would have been much more economical. No wonder she doesn't ask me to come to the airport to receive her – the ever so practical Deepali.* Another fifteen minutes of fidgeting around near the exit gate and he spotted her walking out, the overnighter in tow like an obedient pug guided by its leash.

"Wow, that's a pleasant surprise. What are you doing out of

your bed so early?" elation, scorn, mockery, her statement could have meant just about anything. "I was missing my baby, so I thought that instead of waiting for her in the bed I should come here and shorten the wait," he said, gently planting a kiss on her cheek and reaching out for her bag. "That's sweet. But I was just gone for a day. What have you been up to that's making you miss me so much?" she enquired with a naughty smirk, looking at him from the corner of her eye, as they walked towards their car in the parking lot.

"Well, just a few things here and there. Let us stop by for breakfast somewhere and I could fill you in. By the way, how did your presentations go?"

"The presentations were ok. A pretty hectic schedule though. Can't we skip breakfast and head home straight? I had to get up in the middle of the night to board the flight and am dead tired. God only knows why they had to build an airport in the middle of nowhere. It takes more time to reach the new Bangalore airport from the city than it takes in the flight to Mumbai. I will quickly fix up something to eat at home..." Deepali was understandably and visibly tired and empathetically Akash steered the car towards their apartment. *The breakfast can wait till another day.*

"Yesterday I surfed a bit and also spoke to a few brokers about a rental apartment in Bandra. We should be able to get a decent

2 bedroom flat in about Rs. 40,000. Want to go and check out a few places later in the evening?" As if his words were straight out of a magic handbook, Deepali was suddenly all pepped up, exhaustion having vanished in thin air not leaving as much as a trace behind. "Yes of course. So that's what you have been up to? I think I should travel more frequently, I like what I come back to," she said, reaching out for him and planting a peck on his cheek. *Darn the steering wheel and the road, I can't even reciprocate. Maybe I should have waited till we reached home before opening my mouth.*

It had been a while since Deepali had been throwing subtle and sometimes not so subtle hints at wanting to shift into a bigger and a better house. "It takes Prachi only 15 minutes to reach office from their new house. Bandra should save you a lot of travel time too, right?" "It would be so much fun to get up in the morning and go for a walk on the sea side, looking at the early morning waves and the sun rise. Hey, did you hear that? Didn't that just rhyme?" "Now that we can afford it, shouldn't we look at shifting to a bigger house somewhere in Andheri West or Bandra? Remember how painful it was the last time your folks were visiting? Sleeping on the living room floor and having to walk in the house under the constant fear of bumping into something or somebody; just four people and our house seemed as crowded as the Andheri railway station."

Thus began the familiar and laborious game of house hunting for Akash, only this time he was not totally in charge. They would scan through internet listings and speak to property dealers and potential landlords during weekdays and visit the short-listed properties over the weekends. "Naah, the rooms are hardly bigger than closets." "They want us to pay 50,000 rupees for staying in the middle of these slums?" Deepali had no desire to compromise on her expectations and her blunt honesty continued to slice through the expectant hearts of the dealers – frustrating and at times discomforting Akash.

"I don't know what you are looking for, but we can't exactly rent out a palace for the kind of budget we have. We will never be able to shift if you continue to reject houses because the windows are too small or... or the neighbor owns a dog," his frustration would every now and then surface, rupturing the veneer of his composure.

"There is no need to exaggerate. I haven't said no to any house because the neighbor has a dog or a cat or an elephant for that matter. The windows in that house were hardly any bigger than peepholes; no cross ventilation. You can stay in a sty if you wish to, I can't," she would respond, matching every exaggerated syllable with one of her own.

Like a divine miracle and before the tempest could acquire calamitous proportions, they came across a flat on Hill Road,

Bandra which complemented both Deepali's expectations and Akash's finances. A two bedroom flat, in a relatively new and discerningly well kept complex and the clincher – a small balcony adjoining the living room. It wasn't exactly sea facing, but a stretched walk could lead them to the Carter Road promenade, which offered a picturesque view of the boundless expanse of water and housed a flurry of small stalls and coffee shops, each serving a unique assortment of culinary delights. "An early morning walk by the sea followed by a sumptuous breakfast at *Crepe Station*, we are going to have a great time," she would say, the words sounding straight out of a dream.

Realizing dreams is never a simple task and often requires tireless toil and a price to be paid. The price for realizing Deepali's dream came in the shape of an LED television set, a new sofa set, a wardrobe, a bookshelf, curtains and numerous other small items that were essential for living in an up-market neighborhood. By the time they were ready to shift into their new house, Akash's financial estimates had gone completely haywire. *Shahjahan would have been driven by a similar gusto as me when he decided to build the Taj Mahal. If only we had similar resources at our disposal.* Her efforts had not been in vain and finally when the frenzy of shifting subsided and they were somewhat settled, Akash couldn't help but admire the result.

The first weekend after shifting to Bandra, Deepali expressed her desire to have a house warming party. *Once the elephant has passed, so shall its tail.* As if reading his mind, she said, "don't worry, we will not make it an expensive affair. We will invite only a small group of friends and I will cook at home, but we need to have a house warming party, right?" She had recently developed this habit of asking for reassurances she didn't need. *No it is not right. The house is warm enough and my wallet, pretty cold. So, let's not have a house warming party at all – as if I could have said that even if I wanted to.*

It was a small gathering of nine including the two of them. Not wanting to make it a large and unmanageable group, Akash had restricted his invitee list to three of his closest friends at work – Sudipta, Daljit and Gaurav. Being a Friday evening, the four of them had come straight from work and Deepali, who had left office early, greeted them at the door. An hour later, the contingent of her friends from work convened; four of them, three girls and a man roughly the same age as Akash. He was not the kinds to delve into personal matters like age especially when it came to women, but he couldn't help taking note of the fact that though all three girls looked in their early or mid twenties, though a couple of them could have been much older. *It is funny how short dresses, a well sculptured body and a little bit of makeup can reduce a significant number of years from a girl's age. Wonder if I would have looked any younger had I worn a vest and a lungi, strategically folded a few inches above my knee?*

After the initial round of introductions, there was an awkward absence of conversation, both groups preferring to silently munch on the snacks that Deepali had served. Both Deepali and he made attempts at engaging people by asking the guests about their work and sharing anecdotes from the office involving one or more of the people in attendance. "… and the best was our CEO, Pratap's birthday. Sharada here got one of her friends from a radio channel to call him posing as a kidnapper who had kidnapped his wife, demanding an obscene amount for ransom. She had also managed to convince Pratap's wife into giving a sound byte that was played by her friend to convince Pratap of the kidnapping. It was hilarious; you should have heard his voice. I am sure he would have fainted had the hoax not been revealed for a few more minutes. The radio channel continued to play the recording for a good two weeks after that. I am sure he is not going to forget this birthday for a long time now."

It was eventually the drinks that did the trick and before long, both groups had merged into one larger, homogeneous entity. Daljit was at his wittiest best, bringing the house down with laughter at his digs targeting his own Sikh community – an art that he had skillfully mastered over the years. Everyone seemed to be having a gala time, except Sudipta, who was unusually quiet for most of the evening. "Nothing is wrong. I am just a little tired," she had replied to Akash's concerned enquiry before heading to the kitchen to help Deepali in serving dinner. The home made food was delectable and all the guests complimented Deepali on her cooking. Gaurav was the first one to announce his departure and others, as if waiting for a cue, followed suit. By a little after 1.00 a.m., all the guests had left after wishing Deepali and Akash a happy life in their new home.

"Did you notice? Daljit and Sharada seem to have developed a thing for each other. He is even dropping her home on his way back," Akash said, attempting to fill Deepali on the happenings that she would have missed while serving dinner. "Oh, is it? That's nice. He seems like a nice guy. And I also noticed that he wasn't the only one who seemed to be getting attention tonight," she replied in a mischievously suspicious tone. "Who are you talking about?" he quizzed.

"Who else, I am talking about you. You seemed pretty concerned about Sudipta yourself and she could barely take her eyes off you all evening. I am sure you would have jumped at an opportunity to drop her home, if it had come your way," she continued, her tone now a confusing mixture of accusation and mischief. "Have you lost your mind? Why would I want to drop her home? Are you accusing me of something, here?" Akash unexpectedly snapped out. "Hey relax. Why are you unnecessarily reacting?" she said, raising her voice an octave to match his pitch. "I am reacting unnecessarily? And you can go about saying anything you wish to? What do you want me to do, stop talking to all the girls I know?"

"You know this is not true. I have never interfered in what you do or who you are friends with? I was only pulling your leg and you know that. I really don't see the need for you to react," she said, unable to comprehend his sudden outburst. Akash had realized that his reaction was unfounded but something within prevented him from acknowledging this, perhaps his ego. "You didn't sound as if you were kidding, and what do you mean when you say that you don't interfere with the friends I keep? As if I keep a tab on everything that you do. Do I ever ask you who you are speaking with or who all are traveling with you for all your so called client presentations?" he continued, not willing to concede. The argument continued for another twenty minutes, leading from one needless remark to the other, the main point of contention lost somewhere along the way. Deepali eventually burst into tears and backed out, locking herself in the guest room. Akash did not make an effort to reach out to her and headed for the bedroom instead.

She has never stifled me for space and could have been pulling my leg. But she had no right to accuse me like that. I might have over reacted, but she could have said a sorry at least? Arguments, mostly baseless, but a necessity in most relationships – more so, when the opponents in the diagonally opposite corners of the ring carry with them a strong individual identity. There were more serious concerns taking shape in Akash's mind, though momentarily clouded by his agitated state of mind. Why did he react so strongly to a statement that was probably nothing but childish banter? Why had he suddenly started feeling irritable at things that he would have otherwise taken in his stride? Why didn't he feel the need to knock on the guestroom door and stop Deepali from crying? Was this only a one off incident or a result of something larger that their relationship was going through? Was the elixir losing its magic?

The Third Lap – Seizing Control (June '06 to July '07)

The bitter taste of the quarrel lingered along in their lives for a few more days before the need for cordial living overpowered it, slowly but surely erasing its traces. There was no mediation, not even a composite dialogue and just as the words had popped out of Akash's mouth, like a wanton champagne cork, their impact was also summarily ejected from amidst their being. Their married life continued to traverse the myriad occurrences, marred by a sense of tedium akin to the uniform ticking of the arms of a wall clock. Get up, get ready, go to office, return home, have dinner, go to sleep, only to get up again the next morning.

No, it wasn't that this 'one' incident was responsible for altering much in their lives. They still cared for each other, longed to obtain each others point of view on matters of concern and continued with their recreational outings, albeit at a noticeably lesser frequency. The things that had gone missing were the ones of more inconsequential nature – the giddy laughter, the playfulness, the childlike vivacity that their relationship had exuded at a point in time, not very long ago. The innocent and naïve display of affection had succumbed to the larger issues, mostly relating to their respective careers that kept them preoccupied. They were no longer love smitten kids, but responsible professionals, which meant that even their frivolous chit-chat had to be carried out in a poised and dignified manner, whether in the company of others or just each other.

Some of Deepali's actions that he had adored earlier had started to put him off, of late. Sneaking out of the kitchen with dough smeared hands and transferring some of it to his nose on some phony pretext or the other; suddenly collapsing in his lap when he would be watching TV, pulling his face towards her and the mischievous, satisfied smile after she succeeded in robbing the screen off his undivided attention, or the simple request of making a cup of tea accompanied by feeble and exaggerated excuses that were her indigenous attempts at humor

– "my head is bursting and only a nice, hot cup of tea can save me now," she would say. Akash had never voiced his emerging discomfort to these actions, but it must have been his lack of an equally enthusiastic reaction that had led to their gradual dissolution.

The gradual, dimensional shift in their relationship had ensured that the developments remained oblique and did not stand out as a stark contrast to what their life had been a few years back. Just as Akash was oblivious to Deepali's subtly altering behavior, he had failed to take note of the changes that had come about in his own conduct. The craving for returning home from work to spend time with Deepali was no longer as strong as it used to be; the effort required in planning a surprise for her was now practically weighed on a scale of cost and benefit; time was at a premium and a prioritization was required, Deepali was expected to understand. A gradual drift was challenging the endurance of their unified existence, transforming them into two separate beings leading lives of their own, sewn together by a thread called marriage – and ironically, both of them were caught unaware.

The burning passion and internal biological tempest that was earlier marked by an undying hunger for each other had taken the form of an exciting indulgence reserved for times when there was no other burning issue to be addressed. Their physical intimacy, like the emotional one, had taken a back seat, bringing to the fore their individual ambitions and career aspirations. Deepali had recently been promoted as the Head of Strategy Planning for the Mumbai branch of her agency and was leading a three member team. She was already a known name in the advertising world and her expert opinions on the happenings in the industry were often quoted in 'Brand Equity'.

"Did you see the article from the Awards Night in today's papers? We again got the best BTL (below the line) campaign award this year and they have praised the customer insight that went into its conceptualization. My name is also mentioned," she said, a tendon distending at the side of her neck: pride and sense of achievement. "Which paper? I might have missed it." *If this had happened three years back, would she have waited till dinner time to break the news to me? No, she probably would have called me yesterday to tell me about the award and again today about the article. And she possibly would have carried a copy of the newspaper home and thrust it into my face the minute I walked in. Anyways, where on earth is the Dal?* "Can you please pass the *Dal*?" he continued with his contribution to the dinner table conversation, "there is this Brand Plan that needs to be presented tomorrow. I have been working on it all day and it is nowhere near completion. I will work on it for a while after dinner."

By the time he completed his Brand Plan and came to the

bedroom, Deepali was already asleep, a novel lifelessly fluttering under the weight of her hand, open at the page she was probably reading before falling asleep. He gently lifted her hand and pulled it out, relieving it of the burden and placed it on the bed-side table, marking the page that had been open. He then reached out for the light switch and after a quick glance in the direction of the bed, switched it off, carefully negotiating the three steps that led him to his side of the bed in the ensuing darkness. Tomorrow was going to be a long day and he needed rest.

"And just how do you suppose we will get the additional 10% market share in the upcountry markets?" Shantanu was in one of his belligerent moods today and the tone had been set for the rest of the presentation. Akash and his team, which had now expanded to two Assistant Managers, were presenting the Brand Plan for the next year to his boss, the Brand Head. This plan would form the basis for agreement on the sales numbers with the sales team and the allocation of the annual budget for the various activities and promotional campaigns that Akash was proposing.

"We have planned a few tactical consumer promotions and trade activities, the details of which we shall come to," Akash tried to tackle the question through logic. A logical argument is always prone to counter logic and Shantanu was in such a frame of mind, that he would latch on to any excuse to threadbare the presentation. There was no apparent reason for his aggression, it was just an intrinsic trait that his years in the corporate set-up had inculcated in him and Akash considered himself to be lucky if and when he was able to put his point forward without much ado. "And why aren't we looking at an aggressive growth in the urban markets? Most of the growth for us should come in from urban markets with all the migration that is taking place; and not to forget the increasing usage of detergent guzzling washing machines."

"Shantanu, our strategy is to attract first time users in the rural markets and expand our reach to a wider set of...," Shantanu cut him in the middle of his argument. "It is a stupid strategy. You can't prepare a Brand Plan based on whims and fancies. Please rework your numbers and this time try and substantiate your logic with facts and figures. Let us meet at four and re-look at what you have done," he said before storming out of the conference room. *I do have the figures to substantiate my logic, only if you had the patience to listen. Yes, whims and fancies should not form the basis of any plan, but who can explain that to you?* Though his team members were mature enough to see through the happenings, Akash did not take too well to being bulldozed over in their presence - an act that was fast becoming a second habit to Shantanu, a source of warped and sadistic pleasure.

Not having any intentions to confront him again, Akash reworked the plan in line with Shantanu's expectations and this time around no substantiating numbers and figures were sought. "This looks more realistic. A few minor changes and the presentation will be good enough to discuss with the sales guys. Mail it across to me and I shall fine tune it," Shantanu had said. *Yes, fine tune it you certainly shall. Fine tune; by attaching it to a fresh e-mail and circulating it to the Senior Management as your own handiwork.* Yet again, rank had prevailed over logic and yet again Akash had compromised on his beliefs and esteem - draining and strenuous, but an act necessary for survival in a world marred by incompetence and bloated egos.

Akash felt a sense of relief as he left office that evening, looking forward to burning off his suppressed frustrations on the treadmill, but he was far from comprehending the sinister plans and the pre-ordinated path that destiny had charted out for the rest of his evening; his ordeal was far from over. The abnormally heavy traffic, the near accident and the consequent verbal duel with the taxi driver had left him sapped. The icing on the cake was Deepali's indifference, her lack of sympathy and the preachy mannerism. *A moral high ground is not always the best stand to take.* Before escaping into the diversely peaceful world of sleep, he had made up his mind to take charge of the happenings in his life. There were things he could not help and then there were those that he could, it was time now to make things happen rather than waiting and letting time dictate its terms.

The next day in office, he spent some time in updating his resume. He had decided that he had had enough of Shantanu and his idiosyncrasies and the decision was prohibiting him from engaging in any serious work. Driven by an instinct and a desire to remain occupied with something that could keep his mind away from work, he logged on to his Facebook account. It had been some time since he had last logged on and his lack of activity was evident from the numerous updates, posts and friend requests pending for him to review. One of the requests was from Vikram, his old friend from Business School. *What a coincidence. The last time we had teamed up together, I got my first break in the corporate world. And now, here he is again. Is this some kind of an indication?* The two had spoken a few times after their graduation but post Akash's relocation to Mumbai, there had been no contact between them before now.

Eager to learn of his whereabouts, Akash accepted the request and clicked on Vikram's profile. Vikram was still working with the insurance company he had joined from campus. *So much so for the lack of job stickiness among our generation that they keep cribbing about.* Vikram had also mentioned his mobile number on the profile, which Akash dialed on his own mobile and immediately disconnected. The number was now temporarily stored in his last dialed list and he would speak to Vikram once he was done tending to the other requests awaiting his action in the cyber space. "Dude, how are you doing?" he asked when he heard Vikram's voice, finally emerging after the first few lines of a peppy Hindi movie song had played twice over. *Vikram, still his old, colorful self... what a choice for a ring tone!*

"Who is this?" a serious sounding voice responded. "It is Akash here, Vikram. Did I catch you at a wrong time?" he replied, realizing that Vikram would be in office and might be preoccupied. "Akash, my friend, what a pleasant surprise! No, no, not a bad time at all. I am glad you called. Where have you been?" the recognition immediately changed his demeanor to its usual friendly self. The conversation began with hurling of a generous dose of adjectives from both sides, a ritualistic exercise common between friends connecting after a long gap. Vikram was happily married and living in Gurgaon with his wife and a two year old son. *Vikram's son. Wow, I don't believe this.* As mentioned on his Facebook profile, he was still continuing with his first job and was now the product head for the company, reporting to the Marketing Head. *He seems to be doing pretty well for himself. Product head; not bad at all.*

"You know, this might sound spooky but I had just updated my resume and was about to start circulating it, when I came across your friend request. Do you remember our trip to Gurgaon before the placements? You just seem to materialize out of thin air whenever I am looking for a job. I guess I now know what I need to do when you manage to vanish next," Akash joked. "Yes, of course I remember. I have never been turned out of so many offices in a single day. How could I forget? But why are you circulating your resume? You always wanted to work in the FMCG sector, why the sudden need for a change?" he wondered.

"Yes, I have had enough of selling detergents. It is high time I did something more worthwhile for a living," he remarked heedlessly, his frustrations well cloaked. He didn't want to sound disdainful and moreover voicing his dissatisfaction would amount to accepting defeat; something he could not permit himself to do. "So finally your FMCG fever has worn off? What industries are you looking at? There is an opening for a Marketing Services role in my organization; I could forward your papers if you are interested." *Industry, well, anything would do, as long as the job does not require me to operate a blast furnace.* "Haven't really given it much of a thought as yet, but I guess the profile would be more important than the industry. What exactly is this role?" he asked. Vikram's company was looking for a candidate to head the Marketing Services vertical, a role parallel to his own and reporting to the Marketing Head. The Marketing Services head would be responsible for all internal and external communication and public relations for the company. The role sounded interesting and Akash e-mailed his resume to Vikram within minutes of getting off the call.

He was feeling better after speaking to Vikram, relief and expectant anticipation – things would improve soon. *Shantanu could go sell his detergents wherever he felt like. I don't give a damn.* "Daljit? Want to catch a drink somewhere after office?" he felt like celebrating and had dialed Daljit's extension, the one person who was not known to turn down a drink invite. "Yes sure. I was just asking Gaurav the same thing. God knows how he manages to stay indoors on a Friday evening!" They went to 'Zenzi' in Bandra and continued to drink till the bar announced its final order. The relaxed frame of mind had augmented Akash's appetite for alcohol and Daljit was anyways capable of putting a fish to shame when it came to drinking.

It was a little over 2.00 a.m. when he reached home. He had used his set of keys to open the door, not meaning to disturb Deepali, who was sound asleep by now. His dinner plate was laid out on the dining table, which he surrendered to the confines of the refrigerator before changing into his night clothes and sneaking into bed. He checked his mobile phone for any unread messages before placing it on the bed side table; there were none. As he reached out to switch off the reading light on Deepali's side of the bed, he caught a glimpse of her shut eyes, not completely but with a slight fissure – as if preventing a complete detachment from the world around her; their own little world.

His thoughts instantly darted back in time to an evening three years in the past, when he had been unexpectedly caught up with an agency presentation that had stretched way beyond its planned schedule. Deepali had tried to call him a couple of times but he had been unable to take her calls. When he finally left office at 10.30 pm, in the urgency to reach home, he forgot to return her call. He had walked in to find her waiting at the dinner table, the food totally untouched. Akash had apologized, but she had refused to join him for dinner. "I am not hungry, you eat," was all she said, serving him in the solitary plate on the table. It was his refusal to eat alone, that had finally got her around to joining him but she had continued to sulk for the next couple of days.

"How insensitive can you get? You could have left a text message saying you would be late or at least called when you left office," had been her argument. "Do I ever sulk when you get late at work? I would have taken your call or sent a text message if I could. Yes, I missed out on calling you when the presentation ended but that was only because I was hungry and wanted to get back home at the earliest. But what is all this fuss about 'insensitivity' and what not!" Akash had been annoyed at her over reaction but in the larger interest, had refrained from voicing his feelings. And today, as he lay next to Deepali, in a semi-inebriated state, he was unable to decide his preference – the sensitive and expectant Deepali of yesterday or the callous and indifferent Deepali of today.

He heard from Vikram sooner than expected and the next Thursday he found himself in Gurgaon meeting the Marketing Head for his final interview. He had told Deepali about the opening when Vikram had contacted him to schedule the meeting. "No harm in meeting them. Let them extend an offer and then we can figure out what to do. The option to reject the offer is always open, right?" she had said. In the subsequent week the offer had also come about. The financial offerings were substantially higher than what he was currently drawing and more importantly, the designation of 'Vice President – Marketing Services' had a regal sound to it which made the offer all the more alluring. *Whatever happens, it happens for the good. Maybe this is a blessing in disguise and the distance is what is required to bring back the missing spark in our lives.*

"I got the offer letter today. They are offering a 30% salary hike plus time bound stock options," he initiated the discussion with her over dinner. "That's a pretty healthy jump. So, what are you thinking?" her face remained expressionless. "I don't know. Had it been based out of Mumbai, I would have jumped on it, but going back to Delhi… what do you think?" he wanted to take up the offer but at the same time he wanted her to ask him to do so. The issue was sensitive and had to be handled delicately. He didn't want to reveal his cards and become susceptible to any untoward reaction that Deepali might have. He also didn't want her to think that he was too eager to get away from her; therefore, 'talk less and listen more' was the approach to be followed. *Some tricky decisions are best left for others to make or at least not worth sticking your neck out for.*

"The profile sounds decent and if the money is good, I don't see a reason why you should not take it up," she said after a thoughtful pause, "we can see how it goes and then take a call. If the going is good, I can look for an opening in Delhi and otherwise you can look for a job back here after some time." "Yes, but it is not always easy to find a new job, and if the potential employers get a wind that I am looking at relocating, I might not be in a position to strike a good bargain," he argued, challenging and testing her conviction. Deepali, practical as ever, knew exactly what she was talking about. "Well, you would still be negotiating basis your new increased package and not the current one. So, even a not-so-great deal will leave us better off than where we are today. Anyways, most of the players in the Financial Sector are based out of Mumbai, so the chances of getting something here which is in line with your new role in Gurgaon are much higher. But if you really are not comfortable shifting then maybe you can look for something similar here in Mumbai. I am sure it will just be a matter of time before you land a similar offer, if not a better one."

"Okay. Let me give it some more thought and figure out the best possible alternative. I have anyways asked them for a few days to make up my mind and revert with my decision." The decision, had been made much before their discussion concluded, in fact before it had even begun.

Detour – Back To Gurgaon (July '07 to August '08)

The clouds were forming and re-forming a sonata of quirky shapes; the early morning sun playing hide and seek, suddenly appearing with a blinding luminescence before taking cover behind another cloudy patch. Akash nervously flipped the in-flight magazine, alternating his sight between the natural regalia unfolding outside the aircraft window and some equally aesthetic pictures showcased in the magazine. It was a homecoming of sorts from an exile that had lasted four long years. He had been craving for this escape; an escape from the humdrum life being continually robbed of its sheen, an escape from everything that the city of Mumbai stood for – the chaos, the frantic pace of life, an escape from Shantanu and an escape from… no, he didn't want to run away from Deepali, it was not easy to think of a life devour of her commingling presence. *But it is for our own good. It is just a matter of time and before long, we will be together again.* He had found an argument to plug the void that would start emerging within him at the thought of leaving her behind.

Today, as he took the plunge - the final leg of his much awaited escape, he was engulfed by a premonition-like sinking, giddy, ominous feeling. He could feel the gaze of the dark clouds lurking somewhere in the horizon, clattering their thunderous teeth, waiting to strike. He was scared, just like he would be after a terrible nightmare, only this time it was a 'day-mare' and he was wide awake. *It is just the internal inertia; the mind's habitual resistance to change, that is playing silly tricks on me. It is the nervous anticipation of walking into an unfamiliar territory, the fear of the unknown and nothing else.*

Gurgaon had changed. As his taxi raced down the National Highway - 8, pausing briefly at the toll plaza – a new addition; another government pipeline for claiming an additional chunk from the spoils of the large scale commerce that the 'millennium city' witnessed on an everyday basis. He could notice the marked difference in the landscape of the satellite town to the national capital. Sprawling glass buildings reflecting and refracting light in a manner that made him feel like being trapped inside a gigantic kaleidoscope; shopping malls larger than anything he had ever seen, boasting of kilometers after kilometers of floor space; massive residential complexes constituting numerous small housing units, an arrangement more Mumbai-like, than Delhi and the intermittent bungalows, doing their bit to retain Delhi's cultural identity; most of these, having come into existence mush after Akash had last meandered the streets of Gurgaon.

Akash dumped his belongings in the hotel room, *'The hotel too must have come up recently'*, and hailed the same taxi to his new office. The office occupied a total of six floors in two adjacent buildings within a large commercial complex in the heart of the city. As he settled the fare, he called Vikram on his mobile, who rushed down to meet his old friend. After an animated greeting, mostly comprising of a stream of meaningless invectives, Vikram escorted him to the Management Floor, a section that had retained its exclusivity through the luxurious interiors and liberal allocation of space in comparison with the other floors which were relatively cramped. As they walked down the aisle of the Management Floor, he noticed a chain of small cabins to his left and larger ones in front of him lining the other end of the floor. The space enclosed by the L-shaped boundary was filled by cubicles, arranged in a maze like fashion occupied by serious looking faces, some of whom looked up from their monitors to give him a curious glance. "This is where I sit and the next one will be yours," Vikram said, signaling towards one of the small cabins to their left.

"Come, let us see if Ashutosh is in his room," he said with the informed look of a tourist guide as he walked towards one of the larger cabins on the other end of the floor. *The power centers.* Akash had met Ashutosh, his boss to be, during his earlier visit to Gurgaon for his interview. Ashutosh had an intellectual aura about him and his mannerisms strangely reminded Akash of Prasad, his first boss in the previous organization. *A North Indian version of idli-dosa. This should be fun.* Ashutosh welcomed Akash and took him around the floor for a round of introductions before leading him to his new workplace, his own cabin. *Phew, I will be lucky if I am able to remember even half those names. But, my own cabin, awesome... isn't it?*

Over the next few days, Akash spent a lot of time in office with Ashutosh and outside office with Vikram. His predecessor had left without serving his full notice period and Ashutosh had been directly handling the profile while the search for a suitable replacement was on. Now that Akash had joined, he was eager to get the monkey off his back and had been giving him a detailed download of his responsibilities. Vikram had been playing a perfect host, accompanying him for his house-hunting expeditions; dragging him home for dinner and sharing the closely guarded secrets and gossips from work, insights that would normally remain concealed from a newcomer till such time that he had settled down well and had cultivated his own set of sources.

The invite for the formal induction program had come to him a fortnight after he had first stepped into his cabin. By now he was well settled, having taken complete charge of his work and shifted into a furnished flat close to office, bigger than their apartment in Mumbai and at half the rent. "It is a colossal waste of time, the induction. Boring lectures and presentations aimed only at giving the HR folks something to write in their annual appraisals," Vikram had been vocal about his reservations, "you should ask Ashutosh to get you excused from this sham." However, Akash, not meaning to burn unnecessary bridges, had preferred to attend the program instead.

It wasn't half as bad as Vikram had made it out to be. Though the two full days of classroom sessions had left him thoroughly exhausted, transporting him back in time to his B-School days, he had found bits and pieces of useful information in the otherwise jargon infested presentations by the various functional representatives. The group of inductees comprised of 20 to 25 individuals, most of them having recently joined the attrition marred customer service department. A diverse group, made homogeneous by the unity of purpose and an uneasiness perpetrated by the novelty of the surroundings and faces around. Akash had interacted with most members of the group, though at a very superficial level, innately conscious of the years that separated him from the bunch around, most of whom looked to be in their twenties.

The weekend after he had moved out from the hotel to his newly rented apartment, Deepali had come down to pay him a visit. "We required some information from one of our clients here in Gurgaon and instead of relying on a telecon, I thought I would visit them personally. The personal touch always helps in gaining their confidence you see, plus I would get to keep a tab on what Mr. Malhotra has been up to," she modestly underplayed her efforts, sticking instead to her own brand of casually mischievous humor – a flickering glimpse of the Deepali that was. The same night, Akash experienced a longing and desire for her, as strong as the first time they had made love; carnal instincts looming from a tranquil façade of civility, transforming into a bout of unbridled, animal like passion. *The distance has already started playing its part.*

The next couple of days flew by, shopping for items she considered essential in any household and whose invention he seemed to have missed out on; visiting Vikram, whose son had immediately developed a fancy for his 'Deepali aunty', his pronunciation making her sound like a visiting Chinese dignitary; and conversations – lengthy and meaningful, insignificant and pointless. *Tomorrow morning she will go back, back to her world... our world that I have left behind. Can't she stay back only for a few more days?*

The financial services sector in India was booming, competitors thronging on the doorsteps of potential customers, presenting arguments to substantiate the superiority of their offerings. Telemarketers were busy dialing unsuspecting consumers day in and day out, offering everything from affordable loans to investment plans with previously unheard of returns. There was enough action happening in the insurance space as well, and Akash's organization was not left untouched. Introduction of new products and features, campaigns and carefully designed PR initiatives to instill a sense of fear among the unsuspecting commonfolk, the strategy mills were churning ideas to lure people to the world of insurance. Akash had taken up the challenge head on and had gone about his task in a meticulous fashion, delivering all that was expected of him and more with an alarming consistency.

This speeding, whirligig fluster of excitement that the financial services sector was witnessing, one that would be questioned for its very logic in the not-so-distant future, was responsible for the creation of many heroes. It was the combination of having the desired skill set, an insatiable hunger to succeed and being at the right place at the right time that had catapult Akash into sudden limelight. His insights into the urban markets and in-depth understanding of customer communication, skills inherited from his earlier assignments, had made his contributions invaluable to the organizational success.

The most recent brand campaign of the company had done wonders in increasing the recall value of its offerings, further translating into a significant upsurge in the sales numbers. Akash had come up with an emotive campaign that looked at insurance as a necessity to be left behind for the people we love. "I will always be there to look after you," an ailing father told his young daughter from his deathbed, an advertisement that had found fervor with all sections of the society.

Success was addictive and with every taste of it he would yearn for more, working harder with an even higher degree of determination. "Today I discussed a proposal for signing up a brand ambassador; a personality with mass appeal, someone from the world of cinema or cricket. Ashutosh is gung ho about the idea and intends to discuss it with the CEO soon. It might be an expensive affair, but will help us in establishing our brand among the masses," he would enthusiastically share his ideas and achievements with Deepali, over their ritualistic bed time telephonic conversations which had revived itself like the green spurts of a dying sapling post its tryst with the first monsoon spell.

The milestone was just around the corner and was being awaited with great anticipation; the second private player in the country to boast of five million active insurance policies – no mean feat by any stretch of the imagination, a culmination of the unified efforts of over two thousand individuals towards a common cause. And when it was finally achieved, the celebrations had to match up to the enormity of the occasion and so they did. The '5 Million Party', as it was commonly being referred to, was held in the open expanse of the DLF Golf Course in Gurgaon.

A special performance stage had been set-up on one side of the ground and the open area in front of it, had been skirted with counters serving snacks and food, and of course the four strategically placed bar counters which were clearly favored over the others going by the continuous horde of people surrounding them. All the company employees and corporate agents had been invited for the gala celebrations and the attendance would have easily crossed a thousand. The evening began with a brief congratulatory address by the CEO, entwined with deafening cheers from the crowd and soon the stage was handed over to the Pop Diva who had been specially flown in from Bangkok for the event. While the peppy numbers continued to blast away, the crowd disintegrated into small fractions, some hitting the dance floors and others, the bar and snack counters and yet another set of industrious ones looking to utilize the opportunity for networking and mixing up with the people who mattered – a near chaotic ensemble, bound together by the aura of jubilation.

"Hello Sir," he heard someone call out from behind, a melodious voice pitched up to match the decibels of the blaring music. After meandering around for a while, exchanging pleasantries and making their presence felt, Vikram and Akash had found a comfortable spot at a striking distance from one of the bar counters, nursing their drink and enjoying the transition that their otherwise somber colleagues were undergoing, thanks to the informal atmosphere and the free-flowing booze. Akash turned around to come face to face with the source of the voice, a petite girl with sharp features smiling at him. *She looks familiar, but... no, can't place her. All these girls look so different in office, sans the make-up and these designer outfits.*

"Hello," Akash returned her smile, guising his attentive gaze, looking hard for any clue that could trigger a flash of recognition. She was wearing a black one piece dress that ended marginally below her knees, doing justice to her curvaceous figure. "How have you been? It's been a long time," she continued to chat with him like a long lost friend further aggravating his discomfort of conversing with someone whose existence had been erased from his memory. *She is pretty, alright. But who is she? What do I talk to her about? I don't even know her name. Maybe she has mistaken me for somebody else. It is pretty dark and noisy anyways.*

Fully aware that despite his nonchalant body language, Vikram's senses were completely alert to the developments, he decided not to stretch the game any longer and apologetically answered, "I am doing well, thank you, but I can't seem to recall your name. Have we met somewhere?"

"Oh, I am Monisha," she said with an emphasis on the 'o' that was typical to people from the North Eastern state of West Bengal, "Monisha Sen. We had met during our induction program…"

"Yes of course. I am so sorry. How have you been Monisha, and how has the company been treating you?" he said, taking cues from her introduction to continue the conversation and not offend her with his continued lack of recognition. She did look and sound familiar and perhaps he would have even spoken with her during the induction program but that was some time back and he could not recall any of it. *It must be the drinks… or, or… the old age. Gosh, I am going to be 31 soon. Can you beat that?* Their tête-à-tête continued for another five minutes or so, after which she excused herself to join another group of colleagues, not very far away from where they were standing.

"What was her name? She's from the contact center, right? Pretty girl," Vikram enquired as soon as she was out of hearing distance. "She is Monisha, we had met during the induction program. You need another refill?" Akash said glancing at his half filled glass and walking towards the bar counter without waiting for a response. *Pretty, she sure is, but don't worry dude, I am not going to give you an opportunity to pull my leg over this one.* He returned to find Ashutosh giving Vikram a drunken doze of corporate mantras, a discourse that he quietly joined in as another willing listener. So much so for, what was her name, Monisha. Or, was it?

The Penultimate Lap – A Shocking Revelation (August '08 to October '09)

She was making abstract designs with her index finger on the condensation that had formed on the car window. It was well past midnight and the chill in the air coupled with the thick fog had ensured that the traffic on the streets was abysmal. Akash was concentrating hard, using the reflectors on the road side to guide him through the murky miasma that had blanketed the city. His alcohol infested thoughts, wandering from abhorrence and disgust towards the perpetrator of the events he had just heard about, to sympathy and a deep rooted concern for the victim, the petite figure slouched on the next seat, before he wrenched them back to the more immediate concern of keeping the car on its designated path. Monisha was sitting quietly, her eyes rolled away into a mist from the past, carelessly scribbling with her fingers on the window – an involuntary act to remain in physical contact with the present and prevent herself from being swallowed completely by the demons she thought she had managed to lose in the mist.

The '5 million party' had marked the beginning of a relationship that Akash had come to treasure; an unrestrained friendship, free from expectations and motives allowing two people the comfort of being themselves. Within a few days of the party, Akash had packed off their brief encounter in the closet of his memories when he received a 'friend request' on Facebook from Monisha. Her profile picture comprised of half her face – an eye, the part of the nose that adorned the nose ring and a glimpse of red lips partly covered by her dark wavy hair; an enigmatic creation of 'Photoshop' or some other similar application. She had a large list of friends on the network and if her wall posts were anything to go by, she was pretty active there as well. Akash accepted the friend request and to return the gesture, looked her up on 'sametime', the internal chat engine used by the company.

"Hi thr.. Thanx for the FB request", he wrote and promptly got a reply, "Hello Sir, it was nice to find you on FB… and I had no clue you knew so many Bollywood stars... WOW", she would have seen some of his pictures from their star smitten days that Deepali had uploaded on her profile and 'tagged' him. "Not that I know them personally... just some pictures from my days in Mumbai," he replied, not wanting to dampen her excitement - an excitement akin to Deepali's, during her initial days in Mumbai. The brief chat session was followed by a good morning message and a 'thought for the day', she sent him on 'sametime' the next morning. These messages soon became sacramental and the conversations that followed became more casual with each passing day; 'Sir' becoming 'Akash' and happenings at work giving way to more personal topics for discussion. "How often do you travel to Mumbai?" "So, how was your weekend? What all did you do?" "Did you watch the new Shahrukh Khan movie? You must. He is looking awesome."

Monisha hailed from a small village in the periphery of Kolkata and had been earning a living in Delhi for the past three years. She was staying in a rented flat, sharing it with three ex-colleagues from the call center that she was employed with previously. She believed in living for the moment and making the most of whatever life had to offer, an attitude very different from the focused and ambitious Deepali that Akash had met in the very same city, years back. Oddly though, her liveliness and camel like thirst to soak-in every drop of the bliss that lay concealed in the mundane trivialities, continued to remind him of the Deepali he had come to know in the initial years of his marriage. "Yesterday night, I tried to cook a stew out of the recipe book and by the time it was done, two of my roommates had already gone off to sleep. Guess what, we now have enough stew to last us a whole week." He could feel her excitement oozing from the sentences appearing on the chat window. "No, before you start doubting my culinary skills, let me tell you that the stew was an instant hit with all of them," she added.

The chat window had become a permanent fixture on his computer screen during the work day and it was during one such chat session that Akash had mentioned his desire to try out a new restaurant he had heard rave reviews about. "Yes, I have heard so much about the place too. Let's try it out one of these days. Actually, if you are not doing much, we can go there for dinner today itself…," she had casually fixed up the first of their many outings together, something that he himself had been unsuccessfully trying to bring up for sometime, never able to muster the courage to do so. I hope we don't bump into anybody from office here," she had echoed his sentiments with a blunt honesty that came as a refreshing change in the world of constant perception management and one-upmanship that he had become accustomed to. It was this palpable honesty and lack of guise that was to form the basis of their relationship in the times to come. "Sitting in Pedro's… sipping on red wine… a perfect way to toast another passing day," she had updated her 'status' on Facebook using the application on her mobile phone, sitting across the table from him.

This was about the time that the financial services industry in India had started to feel the heat of the global meltdown, the beginning of one of the nastiest recessions that brought the soaring spirits and incessant optimism to a screeching halt. A host of banks, fund houses and insurance companies had invested heavily in the US real estate market, an investment that had yielded handsome returns till the sector was in a booming phase. Once the downslide began, the property prices came crashing down and most of the properties were left with a value significantly lower than the mortgage amount that had been sanctioned against them in better days. A spate of defaults followed, leaving the investors with properties which had no takers and were priced at less than half the amount that had been written off as defaults against them. The trigger of the global recession saw a host of financial giants filing for bankruptcy or being bailed out by their respective governments.

Akash's company also had a reasonable amount of investment in the US real estate sector that went bad. The situation was not as grim as some of their other competitors and the losses were more than offset by the profits the company had made in emerging markets like India, but the customer confidence had suffered a severe jolt. Skepticism was the order of the day and any organization that was linked to the US real estate sector was being looked upon as a potential candidate for bankruptcy. In such times, the half informed retail investors were shy of investing any portion of their lives savings with such risky companies.

The global media was instrumental in quickly spreading the paranoia to the Indian markets as well and suddenly the soaring sales numbers came crashing down. A large number of policies were closed prematurely and the balance sheets started bleeding, calling for drastic measures for survival. An immediate repercussion of this was a substantial slicing of the marketing and media budget, resulting in some of the work-in-progress projects being canned. This, coupled with the dreadful news stories of bankruptcies, hostile takeovers and massive job cuts pouring in from across the globe and the in-house rumor mill which was on an overdrive, had made the work environment gloomy and hostile. Perception had gained significance over performance and every individual was eager to prove his worth and retain his job, even if it meant stealing credit or stepping on somebody's toes.

Akash and Vikram would share their frustrations and give each other hope, by contemplating the impact of the alternative steps the organization could take to herald itself out of this crisis.

"I don't think that shutting the Indian operations is an option that they would be looking at. Most of the western markets are saturated and the low insurance penetration here is an opportunity for the future that they would not want to let go. However, the talk about downsizing and pruning of the management team might be true," he would share his reservations and Vikram in turn would counter them through his own logic and bits of information, "Yes, but Marketing is safe for now. I was speaking with Ashutosh and he also hinted at some job cuts in sales and operations but categorically stated that there is nothing for us to worry about."

Once back from office, Akash would relay the day's happenings to Deepali, trying to sound optimistic using some of Vikram's arguments to present the situation in better light than it actually was; an act meant to soothe his own nerves rather than comforting her. The situation with Deepali was no different. Clients with depleting profits meant decrease in the quantum of work, renegotiation of rates leading to even thinner margins and irregularity in payments for the work that had already been done. An ascetic cost cutting drive, including a travel freeze for all employees 'unless absolutely necessary', had prevented her from paying him a visit for over two months now. "Good you decided to change sectors; we have at least managed to hedge our risks. God forbid if we were still working for the same company," she, like always, would attempt to counter the despair with a touch of humor clad optimism.

It was in these trying times that Akash longed for Monisha's company. A girl in whose life the only visible impact of the global recession was the reduced clientele at the discotheques and bars in Gurgaon. Her juvenile troubles, mostly stemming out of the three potential suitors who had managed to congregate in her life at the same time, would make him forget his own woes. "Jason read a few posts from Rohit on my Facebook profile and since then he is acting weird. I don't know if he will still be coming to India during his summer break. I am thoroughly confused, he is... I don't know, too possessive." Jason was an Indian student, studying in Melbourne, whom she had met online. During his last trip to Delhi, they had met a couple of times and he had wasted no time in coming up with a proposal. "It was too early, so I told him that I can't commit anything and if he is willing to wait, we can see where it goes," she had clarified her stand.

Rohit was someone she knew from her previous workplace and who had been voicing his interest in her since the time they had first met. Then there was Fardeen, a comparatively recent addition to the list, a friend of one of her flat mates. "No chance. He is a nice guy and all, but not my type," she would say about Fardeen with a conviction that sounded as hollow as the inside of a drum. He was actually the luckiest of the lot and seemed to be getting most of her time and attention. "He is just a kid," and in the same breath she would add, "He has such a long list of girlfriends that I have nicknamed him 'the slut'. But he claims that since he has met me, he hasn't made out with any of them." Her description of Fardeen would tout him as a womanizer prowling the streets of Gurgaon, more than willing to hop on to anything in a skirt that came his way. It certainly was a dangerous liaison that could leave her hurt and tainted. "Don't you trust me? We are only friends and you don't need to worry your brains out over him. I am not at all interested in having a relationship with him," she would respond when he voiced his concerns.

"They should give you the Nobel Prize for communal harmony," Akash would take a punt at her and solicitously add, "You have plenty of time on hand so don't think too much and let time take its own course. If you try to rush into a decision before it is actually due, it will only lead to more confusion." "I don't know. It is all so confusing. Sometimes, I wonder if I will ever get the right guy to get married. The thought of growing old alone and watching other old couples share ice-cream on a park bench is not really comforting," she would dramatize her plight and Akash would be forced to smile at her naivety. A pretty girl, all of twenty three, worrying about being lonely some forty years down the line was absurd, to say the least. "Don't worry that won't happen. And if it does, I will buy you an ice-cream and we can share it on the park bench."

Monisha and her fairytale world, was like a breath of fresh air to Akash and her adolescent vulnerability made him feel a sense of responsibility and protectiveness about her. "Check with your parents, if they are willing to put you up for adoption, there is a ready taker available in me." She would hum and haw about things that would transport Akash back to his teens, a revival of sorts from his otherwise dreary and monotonous life. "She is such a sweet little thing. You must meet her when you come to Gurgaon next," he would add while telling Deepali about one of their outings.

These outings had become an escape from reality for him and he got down to planning the next one as soon as one got over. Mostly she would readily agree, leaving him in a state of elation. *She also likes spending time with me. I am as important to her as she is to me.* However, when she would turn down his suggestion citing some engagement or the other, he would find himself grappling with an uneasy sense of rejection. "I am too tired and want to catch up on some sleep this weekend. Let's plan out something next week," he would accept her excuses on their face value but a part of him would continuously look for a slip up from her that would enable him to put on record his dissent.

A Facebook update or the mention of a movie that she had seen over the weekend, anything that on further probing revealed that she had met up with Fardeen or Rohit would leave him feeling hurt. "You could have told me that you were planning to meet Fardeen this weekend and hence didn't have time to go out with me," he would speak out. "It wasn't planned. He just came to my apartment complex and called me up. Since I wasn't doing much, I decided to tag along," her justifications, a metaphoric acknowledgement of guilt, would make him feel much better. She would be nice to him after every such incident and reinforce his importance in her life by statements like, "Don't you think it is funny how we got talking and eventually became such good friends?" or "You know what I like about you the most? The fact that you tell me things the way they are and not the way I want to hear them." Akash would be euphoric and would express his joy by taking her out shopping and buying her expensive gifts, an attempt to pamper the 'sweet little thing' who was teaching him to live life all over again.

Today was the first time that Monisha had taken the lead to ask him out for dinner, "I am just a little disturbed and wanted to speak to you," she had added. Akash had tried to enquire about the reason but her outright refusal to discuss anything on 'sametime', had made him resign to waiting till the evening to quench his curiosity. Monisha had suggested that they go to Earth Lounge, a quaint and exclusive lounge bar in the outskirts of Gurgaon, a place they had visited a couple of times in the past.

"The music is not too loud and it offers you the much needed privacy to have a decent conversation," she had said. The inquisitiveness was building within him and the venue hardly mattered. The place was usually quiet during weekdays and they had no trouble finding a comfortable seat away from the prying ears of the few guests who were occupying some of the tables.

"Have you heard about the seat rationalization they are planning for the contact center?" she began. *Oh, so this time it was not about another unwanted twist in her blooming love life. The matter was indeed serious.* 'No, what is it about?" he enquired, half expecting what was coming. "There are rumors that they are planning to sack some 200 employees from the contact center due to the reduced call volumes and I have got some hints that my name might be on the list," she said, looking up to him in anticipation of some reassurance. Retrenchments were usually planned under closed doors and Akash was not privy to any such discussion. However, given the conditions, a step like this could not be ruled out. In fact, it was only a logical extension of the cost cutting drive. He found himself struggling for words and in the end could only utter an "oh, is that so?"

"There are no jobs available in the market and I really don't know what will happen to me if I am out of this one. I haven't saved enough to help me last without a job for more than a month and I can't even look at any kind of help from my parents," she was on the verge of tears and it took a lot of reassuring from Akash to stop them from spilling out. "Don't worry, we will find a way out. Let me check on this tomorrow and worst case, even if it is true, I can speak to my friends in other companies and get you a job. I promise that you will not be left jobless for even a month, trust me." Monisha had already burst her usual cap of two drinks for the evening and was still going strong; conceivably a result of her distraught mindset. Akash could not recall any reference to her parents since he had known her. This was the first time she had spoken about them and he was curious to understand the reason behind the scorn with which she had denied the possibility of them being there for her, in her time of need.

"Let it be. I don't want to talk about it. I came here on my own and I need to fend for myself," she had declined to offer any clarifications to his queries. As the evening progressed, the alcohol had it effect, softening her stand, and when she did bare her heart out, Akash was aghast at what he heard. As her words unfolded a ruthless saga of inhuman brutality, he was left in a state of shock, unable to believe that this diminutive soul had been subject to atrocities, that he shuddered even to listen.

Theirs was a normal middle class family, a father working as a driver with the state transport corporation, an elder brother who had managed to break the shackles of life in a small village and moved to Dubai in search of greener pastures and a mother who had been masterfully running the household with the limited resources at her disposal. The first time it happened was when Monisha had just enrolled in the local degree college; she would have been nearing 18 at that time. It was late in the night and she was sound asleep when an unknown sensation and a series of movements pulled her back into reality. She had woken up to an overbearing figure entangled to her body, feeling parts that had never been exposed to sunlight. She had wanted to scream, but a strong hand clasped on her mouth prevented her from doing so. Once her eyes got accustomed to the darkness, she recognized her father's burly figure, stark naked – devoid of even a shred of clothing and reeking of country made liquor. "Relax, it is nothing," he had tried, in vain, to coax her into giving in to his fiendish motives. Unable to counter her continued resistance, he had eventually left her to her own peril and disappeared in the darkness clutching on to what she assumed to be his 'lungi'.

Monisha had remained awake for the rest of the night, fighting an unmatched hatred and loathing for someone she was genetically designed to love and respect. She was old enough to understand the cataclysmic impact this incident could have on the family and her mother in particular, hence had decided to keep it concealed like a nightmare that had never happened, a decision she would live to rue for the rest of her life. "It did not just end there. He started visiting my room regularly, always drunk out of his wits, till I was left with no strength to resist," she said before erupting into another flurry of tears. *She needs to let it out of her system. The tears need to flow.*

"It continued for about two years and I kept facing it without uttering a word. Whenever I went up to my room, I would be scared, dreading his arrival. Sleep had started to elude me and only when he had left my room and I knew that he wouldn't come back, I would be able to close my eyes," she continued digging into her memory, painting a picture as austere as any. "She knew about this all along. Initially I thought it was my own inability to look her in the eye that had stained our relationship but my mother had started to treat me with a contempt that one reserves only for their sworn enemies. She had also resigned to her fate and had found a comfortable scapegoat in me to blame for her plight. Somehow I understand her predicament and don't exactly blame her; she was never strong enough to be able to confront him. Finally when I got my graduation degree, I knew instantly that it was my ticket to freedom and I no longer had to bear sleepless nights scared of the same person whose caress I had longed for during my childhood. Without informing them, I applied online for all kinds of jobs and with a few interviews lined up; I packed a small bag with some necessities, took some money from where I knew my mother accumulated her savings and boarded a train to Delhi."

There was not much left for Akash to say. He quietly settled the bill and escorted her to the parked car. The chill of the Delhi winters was nothing compared to the one he was feeling in his spine and as he dropped her off, he knew that there was a reason why he had met this girl. She needed to be looked after and cared for, and he had been chosen for the task. *You have been filling a deep void in my life and now it is my turn. Nothing under the sun can force you into unemployment till the time I continue to breathe.*

The Last Lap – A Confused State (November '09 to January '10)

It took some careful manipulation on his part, but in due course Monisha got her transfer letter, a key to the much coveted 'Management Floor'.

"I don't think it is a wise idea to ask for an additional head count in times such as these," Ashutosh was not in favor of adding another member to the Marketing Team. "It is only an Assistant Manager position, shouldn't increase the departmental expenses by much. Plus, I really need some support with all the data work that is required for the customer retention strategies we wish to drive. Since the prerequisite for the role is only a basic knowledge of 'Excel', we can hire someone from the contact center redundancy list. HR should also not have any problem since it would only mean one less disgruntled employee for them to handle." His persistence had paid off and Ashutosh sent the requisition to HR. The opening was posted on the internal job site for the company and among a host of yearning aspirants, Monisha applied for it. Some candidates were short-listed and interviewed; a mere cover-up for an inexorable arrangement that had started the cycle in the first place, and the results were declared. Monisha had been spared the horrors of unemployment.

"Oh, so you have finally pulled her over to your team," was Deepali's reaction when she heard about Monisha's transfer. *She can't even imagine the brutality the poor girl has been subject to. Monisha surely deserves all the happy moments that life can offer her in return for all that has been snatched away.* "She was on the redundancy list and would have been asked to leave within a month anyway. Plus I needed someone with similar skill sets, it just made practical sense," he had consciously omitted mentioning the labor that had gone behind carving out a position expressly for her.

From the very first day of her transfer, Monisha had maintained a curt and formal disposition towards Akash in the office. "We don't want people to engage in unwanted gossip," she had explained during the lunch treat she had taken him out for.

This concern had surfaced in Akash's mind too and he was only glad to let her settle it for him. *Friendship is a major deterrent to a successful boss-subordinate relationship. It is best that all matters, not having any obvious linkage to the workplace, are left beyond its boundaries.*

Though their chat sessions continued unabated, the frequency of their out-of-office jaunts suffered a noticeable set back. Akash had tried using the confines of his cabin for informal chit-chat but it simply hadn't worked. He had not been able to let go of the decorous conduct that the workplace demanded and each time he dismissed Monisha with a fresh data request scribbled on her notepad. *It has been a while since we went out, but I guess the risk of someone noticing us leaving office together is not worth it. I will try and catch up with her over the weekend.*

Why do we necessarily need to meet outside work? She is around for most part of the day anyway.

Wonder what gift she finally gave Fardeen for his birthday? It would be too prying to talk about it on 'sametime'; I shall check with her when we go out next.

The impersonal surroundings had suddenly deprived Akash of the beautiful feeling of creating a friendship that would last till eternity; small actions that could impress her into liking him even more; making up for the years that he hadn't known her. Monisha, on the other hand, seemed to be in perfect harmony with the way things were; no hint of discomfort at not being able to spend enough 'personal' time with him, no visible effect of the absence of his proficient advice in matters concerning her adolescent heart, nothing in her life seemed to have changed.

Was it that expectations had started creeping in, once their friendship had evolved to its current form and were his unmet expectations responsible for making him think overtime? Or was it just the fact that the recently established professional relationship was prohibiting her from taking liberties with him that she, as a friend, could comfortably take? Was she suffering from some deep rooted intimacy problem due to which their growing friendship had sent her into an emotional tailspin, making her unceremoniously recede? Or did he never really matter to her as much as she did to him? Though he witnessed her petite shape, her uncomplicated mannerisms, her joys and her sorrows from a greater proximity than ever before, Akash was missing his 'sweet little' friend – she was lost somewhere amidst the impersonal maze of corporate beings.

The first signs of turmoil that this professional extension of his friendship with Monisha would beget into his life, were soon staring Akash in the face. While passing her workstation or while visiting her desk for some work, he would often find her typing profusely, looking at the 'sametime' window on her screen, supporting an involved smile that one would reserve for the happy ending of a feature film. *I am certainly not on the other line and this surely isn't an official conversation. Now, I don't smile like that when I am messaging a data request to someone in the operations team, do I? Who is it that she is chatting with then?* 'Neil' - he had caught brief glimpses of the same name, the couple of times that Monisha had been a fraction late in minimizing the window or cloaking it with another open document. A consultation with the online directory confirmed that the only person going by the name Neil, employed with the company was the young IT Manager who occupied one of the workstations on the Management Floor. Akash had never taken enough interest in him to go out of his way to figure out his exact job description, but his role certainly did not warrant such degree of involvement in anything that Monisha could possibly be working on. *Could he be the reason why she has suddenly become so indifferent towards me? Is there something going on between them?*

Akash could not fathom the genesis of his own thoughts. *Even if something is on between them, why am I bothered? At this age she has every right to mix up with boys her own age. Alright, he is not exactly her age, but so what? I am sure he is an eligible bachelor.* A part of him argued the futility of such thoughts, to be quickly consumed by a part that was pained by a feeling of betrayal. *If something is indeed going on between them, why didn't she tell me about it? I am her friend after all, somebody she kept no secrets with. Wasn't that what she used to claim?* The need for a distraction from this internal tussle made him turn to his books till such time that the static nature of the medium became incapable of containing his thoughts. It was the interactive world of cyberspace that finally came to his rescue, keeping him engaged interacting with long lost friends and discovering new ones. It was on one of the chat sites that he met Neetu, a thirty something, divorcee from Chennai and they clicked instantaneously. She had a knack of telling him just the things he wanted to hear and the shield of anonymity enabled him to share those feelings with her that he had trouble accepting even to himself. "Instead of holding it within you, why don't you just talk to her? For all you know, you might be fretting and fuming over something that isn't even worth a second thought," Neetu suggested when he confided in her about his feeling of being cheated.

It was eventually the sight of Monisha and Neil having lunch together in the office canteen that made him decide to take the bull by its horns. Akash had skipped his breakfast that day and had managed to convince Vikram to join him for an early lunch. As he pushed open the door, a familiar garish laughter followed by the image of Neil and Monisha sharing a light moment over lunch greeted him. His eyes locked with hers for a brief moment, in which he thought he saw a glint of guilt, before he followed Vikram to the counter; a thought that immediately made him feel lighter, like a drug prescribed by an able physician.

"Do you have any plans for the evening? Want to catch up for dinner at Italiano?" he checked with her over the one remaining lifeline of their relationship, 'sametime'. "Sure, it's been a while. Let me know what time and I will meet you there directly." Her reply was not flavored with any kind of guilt, but Akash was not surprised. *She readily accepted the dinner invite, maybe because she wants to tell me something...but that Neil... (Sigh)...I am sure she could have found someone better with her eyes tight shut.* Akash put on a garb of indifference through a better part of their dinner, waiting for her to speak and speak she did.

She talked about work, about the things that she bought during her latest shopping spree, about her flat-mate who was getting serious with the guy she was dating and a host of other things but for the one thing that Akash was longing to hear. "You have been hanging around with Neil quite a bit. Interesting guy, huh?" Akash continued in his flavor-of-the-evening indifferent tone. "Neil and interesting?" she burst out in her trademark uninhibited laughter. "I only wish he was a tad more interesting. I am forced to tolerate him because there is hardly anybody on the floor who I can dare to speak freely with," the conversation slowly drifted away to the analysis of the people who comprised the floor. Her honesty was poignantly touching and Akash felt like a can of garbage for having doubted her at all; and a sense of mysterious relief. *Thank you, Neetu.*

"You are sounding unusually chirpy today," his unburdened state had managed to expose itself to Deepali within the first few sentences he spoke during their telephonic conversation later that evening. *Stupid 'ME' can't help over-intellectualizing every darn thing that's happening around me.* He resigned himself to the overbearing need for sleep thinking about Deepali, their happy times together, the small pleasures that had meant the world to him; the one name however, that remained absent from his thoughts was Monisha's – a name that had left him twisting and turning on the same bed, mutely wrestling painful emotions of his own conjuring, over the past couple of weeks. He was no longer subconsciously sleuthing Monisha's actions at work, a glimpse of an open 'sametime' window on her screen, was no longer a conspiracy that was being carved against him and her casual smile shifted from that of a wily conspirator, to that of a friend he knew everything about.

The normalization of his relationship with Monisha created room for him to think about other things that had eluded his awareness, one of them being his approaching birthday. *31 years! I have lived almost half my life and there is so much more to do. Thank God that it is on a Sunday this year. I might be able to make a quick trip to Mumbai. Deepali will be pleased.* He had broached the idea of a weekend visit to Mumbai but Deepali was to travel to Bangalore for a client meeting, a dead-end even before he had started planning. *I am sure she hasn't forgotten my birthday, but postponing an important client meeting might not be a wise idea. We can always celebrate later.* He was no stranger to the bits of sacrifice that a successful corporate career demanded and completely understood and empathized with her predicament. *Plus I can do something to keep myself occupied. Maybe a nice dinner somewhere with Monisha... She might be planning one of her amateur surprises for me, like she had done for Fardeen's birthday.*

Friday had been an unusually busy day for Akash and he had only managed to fire his last e-mail out at 10.15 p.m. before heading home. The peak hour traffic had long dispersed and in no time he was parking his car in the allotted parking space of his apartment complex, unaware of the surprise that patiently awaited him. As he opened the main door, still mentally engaged with the work that he had left behind, he felt as if he had suddenly walked into a completely different world. A bunch of fragrant candles and the resultant shadows, their fragrance mixed with that of home made condiments which were tastefully laid out on the dining table, and Deepali – her movements artistically captured by the candlelight reflecting from her silver one-piece dress and the changing shapes on the wall, as she reached out for him. Akash was on the verge of tears. The Bangalore trip had been an excuse for her to be able to execute her own plan. *Why couldn't I see through it?* The delight of the unexpected, coupled with Deepali's assiduity, had left him speechless, but words were anyways not going to be of much importance for the remainder of the night. The untouched food, which would serve as their lunch the next day, was a testimony to the actions of immense longing, love and unheralded passion that had negated any need for the use of words.

The next day had a lazy start with neither of them managing to tug out of the bed till late in the afternoon. Their evening had been spent in a few of the many shopping malls in Gurgaon and at the stroke of midnight, when Akash completed 31 years of his existence on earth, they were nicely cuddled up on the sofa, watching a movie on television and sipping red wine. It was when Deepali wished him for his birthday that the next surprise was revealed, a Tag Heuer watch that he had seen in one of the malls earlier in the day. *I had only glanced at it once, not stopping to even ask its price. How did she know that I had liked it? Also how did she know that I wanted a new watch? It must have cost a bomb though... I was with her all the time, when did she manage to purchase it?* The next one to wish him was his mother who called him at a few minutes past twelve, a ritual that had been going on for as many years as he could remember.

Akash continued to fiddle with his phone till the movie ended, but barring a couple of text messages from his colleagues there were no other wishes that came his way.

The next evening, Deepali invited Vikram and his wife for dinner. Vikram's son had conveniently forgotten his 'Deepali aunty' and she had to make efforts to refurbish the bond they had established during their last meeting. The child and his adorable actions, the drinks and the happy occasion, all added to the cheerful evening; except for Akash, who every now and then would slip into thoughts of his own, only to be brought back by a question or a statement warranting his attention. *The day is almost over and she hasn't even wished me. Could she have forgotten? No, she had been discussing Fardeen's birthday gift a week before it was due. She is not the type to forget her friends' birthdays. But then why hasn't she called? Or even an SMS...* It was not that he wasn't having fun or was not happy to have Vikram over but just the fact that he had no control over his thoughts, which, like a pendulum, were swinging between the happy moments of the present and a complex algorithm of possibilities that his troubled mind was conjuring. Just when he had been dragged to the present once again by a glass that Vikram's son had dropped, his mobile phone rang. 'Monisha', the name flashed on the screen as Deepali picked it up from the side table and handed it over to Akash.

"So, you remembered?" he sarcastically enquired, once she was done singing an animated version of a Hindi movie song, wishing him a life of 1000 years and each of those years having 50,000 days – a song having no semblance to the average life expectancy of humans; perhaps inspired by the age of dinosaurs, literally and metaphorically. Akash walked to the bedroom and shut the door behind him, an act that could pass as polished mannerism but was driven more by the need for privacy and the need to be able to vent out his feelings that had been surfacing sporadically all through the day.

"You thought I would forget?" she replied, completely ignoring his mordant tonality. "Well, I was hoping you would call earlier. I saw you planning Fardeen's birthday gift with so much affection and passion that I assumed you would be doing the same with all your friends," he replied sarcastically, a tinge of jealousy creeping into the dialogue – a feeling that he had been wrestling with all day. "Why are you even comparing yourself with Fardeen? I couldn't obviously ring your doorbell at twelve with a bunch of flowers and some silly cards, screaming 'Surprise' at the top of my voice? That would have been so silly... so childish. You are more important to me than all the Fardeens of the world and I wanted to get you something special for your birthday. I have been thinking about it for a while and finally I know what to get you. It will take some time for me to complete it, but I think the wait is going to be well worth it."

"But you could have at least called earlier to wish me? I thought you had forgotten about my birthday," her explanation had yet again proven to be the answer to all his self-inflicted anxiety and within seconds he was back to being his normal self. "Don't be silly. How could I forget your birthday? Just that I had left my charger in office and my phone had been out of battery since Saturday morning. Right now also I am calling you by using my SIM card in my roommate's phone." The conversation soon shifted to his birthday gift that Monisha was preparing but despite all his attempts she didn't give him any clue as to what it might be. After about 15 minutes, a happy and cheerful Akash emerged from the bedroom to join the others in their merry making.

Monisha's vivacity and zest for life, the vulnerability arising out of her simple and straightforward outlook, had made him take upon himself the task of protecting her, being there for her when she needed him the most. Her endearing existence had painstakingly cast upon him a magical spell, so obscure that she herself was probably unaware of having worked it. His love for her was not completely selfless though. He did expect some degree of importance and inclusion, which at times her uncomplicated view of life deprived him of, propelling him into an all-consuming mental whirligig. *She is too immature to be able to manage expectations and do things to make others happy. She does acknowledge that I am an important part of her life and shouldn't that be enough?* The answers to his mental agony were always simple, so simple that he would not even have touched upon them during his internal deliberations and when she stated them just as simply, he would be left blaming himself for all his suffering. The periods following each such realization, were the happiest, with Akash managing to bury all his expectations, at least momentarily, and Monisha making an effort to reiterate his importance in her life.

The bliss continued for over a month after his birthday. The 'Gift' that she had mentioned was a pencil sketch of his that she had made herself. "I used to do a lot of sketching while in school, but this is the first one I have made in the recent times," she said when Akash unwrapped his belated birthday gift. It wasn't exactly something that would have made Leonardo Da Vinci proud, but Akash's features were recognizable and someone looking at him and the sketch together could tell that they were intended to be the same person. It was not the resemblance but the time she would have spent making the gift with 'her own hands', that made it his most treasured possession. The Tag Heuer watch came a close second. "Are you by any chance falling in love with this girl?" Neetu had enquired when he shared his excitement at finally receiving the much awaited gift. *LOVE, she must have lost her mind. It is not her fault though; selfishness has become so deep-rooted in our lives that we have become incapable of accepting the existence of a selfless friendship, not marred by the designs of attraction, emotion or otherwise.*

It was one evening of this 'happy' phase when Akash was returning to office after a brainstorming session with the agency that he saw Monisha on the other side of the road, perhaps waiting to hail a shared cab to take her back home. Akash steered his car to the side lane and drew his mobile phone out of his pocket as the vehicle came to a complete stop. *Let me ask her to cross over and I will drop her home. We can also grab a bite somewhere on the way.* Searching for her name in the address book, he glanced towards her to check if she had seen him stopping. She hadn't. Instead, she was mounting on the pillion seat of a motorbike; the rider, despite the helmet concealing his face, was unmistakably Neil. Akash retired the mobile phone to his pocket and proceeded with his original plan to go to the office.

Neil...but I thought he was just someone she had been hanging out in office for the lack of other options. Where is she off to with him? Once in the confines of his cabin, he intuitively repossessed his phone and dialed her number. The ring continued unabated before a recorded voice told him that his call had not been answered, a fact that he had obviously noticed. *He might have offered to drop her home and she obviously would have preferred a ride with him than waiting for a shared taxi. She would not have heard the phone ring and it is not easy to have a conversation while sitting on a motorbike. She will call me back once she reaches home.* She called him back within twenty minutes of his unsuccessful attempt.

"Hi Akash, you were trying to call?" He could hear Shakira's voice loudly, pronouncing the truthfulness of hips, in the background. "Yes. Actually I was coming back to office after the meeting so wanted to check if you were still here," he replied, concealing carefully the true motive of his attempted call. "Is there something you required?" she enquired. "No. Nothing, that can wait, where are you anyways? There seems to be a lot of noise in the background…" he continued. "Oh, I just bumped into one of my roommates on the way back and we decided to stop by at 'Buzz' for a bite and a couple of drinks.' *But I saw her leaving with Neil. Why would she lie to me?* He could feel the furrow of anger between his eyebrows and hung up before it became impossible for him to continue with the act of ignorance.

Blood was pounding in his temples and he could feel his liver turning into jelly with the palpitation of extreme fury that had engulfed him. *She is blatantly lying and God only knows since when she has been doing this. Has she been using me all this while?* The recently concluded conversation had ruled out any possibility of Akash being able to concentrate on his work and sifting uneasily, trying to stifle the resultant rage, he packed up for the day and returned home. He felt cheated and used, it hurt him badly. *All this while, I thought she was the naïve one. How did I manage not to see through something so apparent? I thought of her as a friend for life and for her… for her, I was one of the many guys doting on her, a source of attention and self appeasement.*

The faceless enemy he had valiantly fought during the turbulent times of their relationship, now had a face; a dusky face with sharp features and pretty eyes. Monisha's innocent face, jacketing the scheming and conniving girl secreted within. Left to his own devices, he would have loved to give her a taste of her own medicine, but that would mean stooping down to the despicable standards that she had set in their relationship and then there was Deepali he had to think about. *What would she think if she ever heard about all of this? And where on earth is Neetu?* Neetu, the one person he could share his predicament with, was offline. A small disappointment, compared to the others he was trying to deal with. He left a long message for her on Facebook, the only vent available for the frustration that was brewing within, stretching him at the seams.

The next morning Akash left his bed with a resolve to put an end to this chapter of his life, a chapter which had so far given him nothing but pain and mental agony. *It has to end and end it shall on MY terms.* He had made a conscious decision to ignore Monisha in the office, depriving her of the pleasure of having succeeded in another craftily executed deceit. *Let her come up to me for a confrontation this time and I shall do something I should have done much earlier – show her the mirror and expose her true self to her.* As the day unfolded, he found it much easier to stick to his resolve than he had anticipated, mostly because of the catastrophic news story in the papers that had left him with no time to even breathe.

'How safe are you?' read the headline in one of the leading dailies. A compact disc, containing the personal details of about five million insurance policy holders had been seized by the cyber crime cell of the Delhi Police; one of the largest breaches of customer confidentiality reported in recent times. The reports had named Akash's company as being the source of data leakage before going on to analyze the larger impact of the incident on the financial services sector as a whole and other ancillary industries like business process outsourcing, which were likely to bear its brunt. 'This occurs just when the financial pundits had started raving about the rising customer and investor confidence in the Indian financial sector. Will this scandal derail India Inc. from its recovery path?' another article had left its readers with a thought to ponder upon.

Akash had immediately sprung into action, trying to contain the damage by keeping his company's name out from any further speculation. Most of his day had gone into drafting press releases, answering media queries, interacting with officers and agencies that were likely to give a favorable byte or two, to dissolve their company's name from a pre-trial crucification by the over zealous media. It was a trying day and Akash had risen up to the occasion, taking control of the situation and doing all that was humanly possible to salvage it. Later that evening, exhausted, he lay on his living room sofa taking stock of the day's events. He had seen Monisha a couple of times during the day but had been too preoccupied to spare a thought for the quandary he had endured at her hands only a few hours back; the thoughts that were now gushing back, taking advantage of the bog of muteness that surrounded him. Scared to let himself drift back into a relapse of his mental state from the last evening, he reached out for his phone – an able distraction. There were three missed calls from Vikram and one from Deepali, blinking for his attention.

As he was pondering over whom he should dial first, the phone started vibrating again. Vikram had made his decision easier. "Akash, where have you been? I have been trying to reach you all evening," an anxious voice greeted him. "I have been home, was a little tired so had left the phone on silent…but why are you sounding so flustered? All well, I hope?" Vikram was known to maintain his cool in the most demanding of situations and that made his current troubled demeanor sound ominous. "I heard that they were tracking the CD back to the system it had been written from and there is some talk that it could have been your laptop," Vikram had his sources that kept him abreast with all the happenings, behind closed doors or otherwise. Only sometimes, they bordered between fiction and reality and this certainly was one of those times.

"Are you crazy? Who told you that?" Akash asked. "No, I am not crazy. Forget about who told me what and tell me, could you have downloaded the data for something and then forgotten to destroy it?" Vikram was in no mood to defend the credibility of his source and was clearly concerned about Akash. Akash paused to think and then confidently replied, "Nay, I haven't accessed the customer database in quite sometime. It must be some misunderstanding and I am sure the IT guys will figure that out sooner or later. You don't worry and thanks for letting me know." "I don't know…I heard that they were pretty sure about the data being downloaded from your terminal and a high level inquiry involving the department heads, is being scheduled for tomorrow…but maybe there is some kind of an error." Akash's confidence had worked well to pacify him and Vikram had eventually hung up sounding reassured. '*An extension of the chain reaction of farcical panic,' thought Akash. It was nice of*

Vikram to let me know but someone needs to take these IT guys to task. They have no business opening their trap before they have their facts in place.

The Finishing Line – A Tryst With Truth (15th January '10 and Beyond)

The first thing Akash did for the day was to scan the morning papers for any follow-up stories pertaining to the 'data leakage' that might have found their way into print. There were none. Akash was relieved. Articles about the solar eclipse, that was to be witnessed later that day had overshadowed the fiasco and were occupying most of the news space, a development that Akash thanked his stars for. The frenzy of the preceding day was missing and Akash quickly settled in his cabin, clearing the backlog of e-mails that he had not been able to attend to yesterday. He was only done with a handful of them, typing crisp replies to some and discarding the others into the trash folder, when a pop-up signaled the arrival of a new message. It was Tina, the CEO's secretary and she wanted Akash to block his calendar for a meeting with the big-boss sometime in the afternoon.

The message reminded him of his conversation with Vikram last night, the thought of which he quickly brushed away. *A lot has happened in the past 48-hours and I have been in the thick of most happenings. The CEO might be wanting to discuss any of those developments with me, and who knows, an acknowledgement of my deft handling of the situation could also be on the cards.* Finally, the time came when he found himself facing the CEO and with him three members of the top management team, questioning him about the data leakage - their stern, gruff, businesslike demeanor making him feel like a convict facing a hostile jury. He found himself being suspected and ostracized, a realization that hurt him deep within. *Vikram was right. I should have paid more attention to what he had to say and maybe I would have been better prepared to prove my innocence.* He knew his pleas sounded as weak as the straw that a drowning man holds on to, hoping for it to land him to the shore.

His mouth was dry, his tongue cleaving to the roof of his mouth, words stuck between his teeth like shreds of chicken, refusing to come out when he so desired. He could feel the floor beneath his feet vibrating, or were his own feet playing a trick on him? He could see his promising career being eclipsed by an act, he knew he was not responsible for, but found himself lacking the strength and the means to prove his innocence. He had been undone and like a bleeding soldier, out of ammunition, he decided to give in to the grip of silence; a silence so absolute that he could clearly distinguish the steady rhythm of his own breathing, from that of the other occupants of the room. The silence, before it could consume him completely, was broken by a steady knock on the door. As the door opened, introducing Tina into the gloom - slowly walking towards Roopam and whispering something, he thought he saw a glimpse of Vikram lurking behind the now shut door. *Hallucinations and what perfect timing. It is about time I was declared mentally unstable.* He watched Roopam get up and follow Tina out of the room – a bleakly ambiguous gaze of a man, too tired to comprehend what he was witnessing.

His trance that continued for an indeterminate amount of time was broken momentarily when Roopam returned to the room. "There have been some developments that I think we need to discuss immediately," he spoke to no one in particular before turning towards him, "Akash, would you please excuse us for some time?" The only thing he could comprehend was the literal meaning of the request and like a zombie Akash got up from his seat and walked out of the door. *Vikram, so he was indeed outside. What is he doing here?* Akash was pleased to see a friendly face but was too disillusioned to ask any questions. Understanding his state of mind, Vikram put his hand over Akash's shoulder and guided him away. "Come," was all he said and Akash complied like a patient under the influence of sedatives being guided to the comfort of his bed by the caretaker. He soon found himself exiting the office compound and walking towards the nearby coffee shop, carefully steered by the man in command, Vikram.

It was when he saw Deepali getting up from one of the corner tables that his senses started regaining control over him. "You? What are you doing here?" he uttered in disbelief. "We will explain everything. Why don't you take a seat first and have a glass of water?" it was Vikram who had replied, while Deepali continued to stare at him blankly. Her presence was comforting. He was amidst friends now and he suddenly felt a new lease of life flowing through him with every sip of water that he gulped down. "Here, this should give you some idea as to why I am here," she eventually spoke, handing him a set of print out's carefully stapled into two different bundles. One of them, he recognized as the transcripts of his chat with Neetu. *Neetu?* But the other was a similar transcript of Facebook messages that he had never seen in his life before this day. It was a conversation between a girl named Jacqueline and a boy who called himself 'wonder boy' (later Akash would recall how he had first read 'wonder boy' as 'wonder bra', adding to his already confused state), both names lacking any kind of familiarity.

Piece by piece, as the saga unfolded, Akash continued to listen with utter amazement and dismay – a story as convoluted as a Chinese puzzle. "It all started when you first told me about Monisha. I noticed the excitement in your voice when you spoke about her and when she became the single most important topic of our discussions, I felt a little uncomfortable. I didn't want to encroach on your personal space and stifle you, so I didn't voice my concerns. I love you a lot Akash and can't bear to imagine my life without you," she used a tissue from the table to wipe the dampness from her eyes. Akash was too stunned to react and quietly waited for her to resume.

"It was when your relationship with her started impacting your behavior towards me that I knew something had to be done. You had suddenly become ornery and distant. I couldn't take it and that was when I created a profile under the fictitious name of 'Neetu' and added you to my friends' list. You would speak freely about your feelings with Neetu and that helped me keep track of what was happening in your life and also advise you in times when you really needed some. As Neetu, I wanted to be there for you at times that you would not want Deepali to be around. Your conversations with Neetu were what made me realize that the girl was taking you for a ride. On your birthday when a phone call from her helped liven up your mood, something that I had been struggling with for the entire day, I felt terrible. I knew that you actually felt for her, cared for her and I didn't want to confront you basis a hunch I had about her. I knew you would not believe me and my intrusion would only draw you further away from me. I had to somehow figure out what she was actually up to and it was you who finally gave me the idea.

When you told Neetu about Neil and Monisha, I knew this was something that required further digging. I created another profile on Facebook by the name of Jacqueline, a vibrant young girl from Mumbai. I took some pictures from one of the many portfolios that are mailed to our agency by aspiring models and uploaded them on Jacqueline's profile. This ensured that when I left a casual message on Neil's wall, he took the bait and immediately added me as a friend. I led him on and asked him all about his love and sex life and in his zest to match up to Jacqueline's gregarious nature, he went on to boast of his colorful and 'ultra cool' lifestyle. Here, you might want to read some of this," she said, pointing out to a section of the print-outs she had initially handed over to him.

Jacqueline: hmm... thts interesting. And who is this girl in office?

Aren't you scared that people might find out?

Wonder Guy: She's recently been transferred to our floor. Apparently her boss has a big time crush on her, so yes, we try and exercise caution.

Jacqueline: that's even scarier... I like your guts...

Wonder Guy: Thanx...

Jacqueline: So, are you serious about this girl?

Wonder Guy: No, I am not. We are what you call Fuck Buddies. I am getting what I want and she what she wants. She knows I am not the commitment types...

Jacqueline: and this boss of hers, what if he finds out about you two? And just how do u know that he has a crush on her in the first place?

Wonder Guy: Oh, he keeps chasing her all the time. Apparently he keeps asking her to meet him outside office and behaves like a spurned lover when he sees her with me. Even if he finds out, there is little he can do to me... at most he can spoil her appraisal ratings and she claims to have taken care of that by some crappy story that she has given him about not having any other friends in office that she can talk with...

Jacqueline: neat man. It is extremely difficult to find such people who believe in living life for the day. My last boyfriend went down on his knees to ask my hand for marriage while I was having a shuddering orgasm… can you beat that?

Wonder Guy: LOL… now that's something I would never do…

The chat transcripts continued but Akash could bear to read no more, a melting realization about things not being the way he thought, dawning upon him. He dropped the sheets on the table, looking up at Deepali, a signal that he had read what she wanted him to read and that she could continue.

"Yesterday evening, when Vikram was trying to reach you and you were not responding, he ended up calling me. He told me about the findings of the IT team and their suspicion that the data had been downloaded from your workstation. This immediately rang a bell somewhere. During our last chat, Neil had been coaxing me, in Jacqueline's avatar, to join him for a vacation in Switzerland. He had even offered to bear all my expenses. I hadn't paid much attention to him then and had ignored it as one of his boisterous drives. But when I heard what Vikram had to say, I was able to put two and two together. I knew you were in trouble and the proof I had was not enough to save you from it. So yesterday night I again chatted with him about the Switzerland vacation. Here," she turned a few sheets from the bundle and pointed out to a section.

Jacqueline: Hey, where did you vanish? Did you get scared that I might actually take you up on the Switzerland vacation offer? ;)

Wonder Guy: No, nothing like that. I have just been slightly busy off late. The Switzerland offer is open… tell me if you can come and I will get the bookings done…

Jacqueline: No man. Switzerland is too expensive. If you want to plan a trip to Goa or something, I am game…

Wonder Guy: Why are you worried about the expenses? I told you, I will take care of that…

Jacqueline: And just where would you get that kind of money?

Wonder Guy: Nothing just a small windfall gain…

Jacqueline: A windfall gain is not enough for a foreign trip… you are not telling me the truth are you?

Wonder Guy: Forget it. Why is the source so important? I have the money and that's what is important… right?

Jacqueline: No, I need to know where the money came from.

Wonder Guy: Why don't you understand? I can't tell you… I might land up in trouble if I did…

Jacqueline: very well then, you can keep your money then…

Wonder Guy: why are you getting upset now?

Jacqueline: well, I haven't met you even once and I am willing to go on a vacation with you… and you don't even trust me enough to be truthful to me and think that I might land you in trouble. What else am I expected to do?

Wonder Guy: It is nothing like that… okay, but please keep it to yourself and don't repeat it in front of anybody…

Wonder Guy: you would have read about the data leakage scandal in the papers today.

Jacqueline: Nope, I might have missed it. What was it about?

Wonder Guy: Well, the story was about a middleman the cops caught trying to sell a CD containing the contact details of 5 million insurance customers. And as for the money, that CD was worth its weight in gold.

Jacqueline: What do you mean? What did u have to do with the CD?

Wonder Guy: Forget it. As I said, it is not important… What is important is that we are going to Switzerland?

Jacqueline: No, tell me more na... plsssss. This is super cool… what did u do?

Wonder Guy: Well, the data belonged to my company and I was the one who got it out…

Jacqueline: wow…that's gutsy… hey, but what if they track it back to you. I mean, u said that the middle man who had the CD has been arrested…

Wonder Guy: It was an anonymous deal and can't be traced to me. The guys I sold the CD to haven't seen me; in fact they don't even know my name. The deal was finalized over e-mails from a fictitious ID and I simply couriered the CD after the money was transferred to a set of bank account numbers I had given them. The bank accounts are also closed now and the money is in my possession. Happy? So, can we plan our vacation now?

Jacqueline: yes… this is all so exciting. But tell me, how did you manage to get hold of the data in the first place?

Wonder Guy: that was the easiest part. Monisha, this friend of mine from office copied the data on to a CD from her boss's laptop.

Jacqueline: and why did he allow her to do such a thing?

Wonder Guy: The idiot trusts her blindly and often lets her use his laptop and data card to access her personal e-mail and other networking sites that are blocked on the office network for security reasons. As always, even this time around, he had walked out of his cabin when she was using his laptop for personal reasons; giving her all the privacy she needed…

Jacqueline: so this girl… she also knows about it? What if she tells somebody?

Wonder Guy: You know what your problem is? You worry too much. She was the one who actually got the data out so if she speaks out, she would be the first to get into trouble. Plus I have already handed over her share to her…

When Akash was done reading, the puzzle suddenly lay threadbare in front of him. Deepali went on to explain how she had called Vikram and told him the entire story yesterday night and had taken the first flight in the morning to Delhi. Vikram had confronted Neil with the print outs that Akash had just read and had threatened him with a copy being handed over to the cyber crime cell. Neil had finally owned up to the crime when Vikram had explained to him that the organization might be happy to let him go with a termination since his arrest would only malign its reputation further. "There is no harm in swindling a swindler. The glimmer of non-existent hope that the buggar saw, made him confess and as a result he is on his way to the lock-up and you are free to sip coffee with us," Vikram added, his good humor unimpaired in the wake of all that had transpired.

The incident had its own lessons for Deepali and Akash and within the next month, he found himself a job in Mumbai and shifted back. They had both realized that the race they were madly running in, led to nowhere and it is only in the company of loved ones that true happiness exists.

It has been over a year now, from the day the moon eclipsed the sun for the longest duration in 100 years, and Deepali and Akash are eagerly awaiting the arrival of the newest member of their family. Deepali wants a small boy who would look and behave like Akash, while he is praying hard for a sweet little daughter. Vikram is still hanging on to his first job and rumor has it that he would soon be taking over from Ashutosh as the

Marketing Head for the company. Neil is still languishing in Tihar Jail and Monisha, whom the court had been comparatively lenient with, vanished without a trace after serving her prison term of three months. The only memory of her that remained with them was a tissue paper on which Akash had been scribbling while Deepali was narrating the story in the coffee shop below his office. Deepali had picked it up from the table and preserved it; it read:

The mighty Trojans fell, and so did I…

A wooden horse you were not, yet in a pool of my own blood I lie.

Dawn follows every dusk…

And all that rises, fall it must.

So my blood shall find its way and trickle down your eyes,

The day your deeds of today eventually make you cry.